学术顾问

（以姓氏笔画为序）

王　宏　　冯智文　　李正栓　　李丽生　　原一川

Academic Advisors

Wang Hong　　Feng Zhiwen　　Li Zhengshuan

Li Lisheng　　Yuan Yichuan

主　编

李昌银

副主编

黄　瑛　　彭庆华

General Editor

Li Changyin

Professor of English Yunnan Normal University

Associate General Editors

Huang Ying

Professor of English Yunnan Normal University

Peng Qinghua

Professor of English Yunnan Normal University

云南少数民族经典作品英译文库
Classics of Yunnan Ethnic Groups in English Translation

主编　李昌银　General Editor　Li Changyin
副主编　黄瑛　彭庆华　Associate General Editors　Huang Ying & Peng Qinghua

Chamu
查 姆

整理◎郭思九　陶学良
英译◎徐蔚　熊莺
译校◎[美]包琼

Edited by Guo Sijiu & Tao Xueliang
Translated by Xu Wei & Xiong Ying
Revised by Joan Cecile Boulerice

云南出版集团
云南人民出版社

图书在版编目（CIP）数据

查姆：汉、英／郭思九，陶学良整理；徐蔚，熊莺英译. -- 昆明：云南人民出版社，2018.12
（云南少数民族经典作品英译文库／李昌银主编）
ISBN 978-7-222-17498-6

Ⅰ.①查… Ⅱ.①郭… ②陶… ③徐… ④熊… Ⅲ.①彝族—史诗—中国—汉、英 Ⅳ.①I222.7

中国版本图书馆CIP数据核字(2018)第277429号

出 品 人	李 维	赵石定
项目统筹	周 祥	殷筱钊
项目组稿	郭木玉	
责任编辑	郭木玉 任建红 李东华	
设计制作	马 滨 三人禾	
责任校对	李智燕 崔苡菡 付芳侠 周桉吉	
责任印制	陆卫华 代隆参	

云南少数民族经典作品英译文库
Classics of Yunnan Ethnic Groups in English Translation

查 姆
Chamu

整理◎ 郭思九　陶学良
英译◎ 徐蔚　熊莺
译校◎ [美]包琼

Edited by Guo Sijiu & Tao Xueliang
Translated by Xu Wei & Xiong Ying
Revised by Joan Cecile Boulerice

出　版	云南出版集团　云南人民出版社
发　行	云南人民出版社
社　址	昆明市环城西路609号
邮　编	650034
网　址	www.ynpph.com.cn
E-mail	ynrms@sina.com
开　本	787mm×1092mm　1/16
印　张	19.5
字　数	280千
版　次	2018年12月第1版第1次印刷
印　刷	云南出版印刷（集团）有限责任公司　云南新华印刷一厂
书　号	ISBN 978-7-222-17498-6
定　价	108.00 元

云南人民出版社
公众微信号

序 一

◎李正栓

　　民族典籍英译是传播中国文化、文学和文明的重要途径，是中华文化走出去的重要组成部分。文化与文学的传播，是一个国家提高文化软实力的重要方式，在文化交流和文明建设中起着不可或缺的作用，对提高国家对外话语权、构建国家对外话语体系以及对建设世界文学都有积极意义。

　　中国各少数民族拥有许多优秀的典籍，具有很高的文物价值、文学价值和文化价值。各民族的先人们通过口头流传或用文字记述了他们各具特色的文化。各少数民族几乎都有自己民族的创世史、史诗和神话传说。

　　中国民族典籍独具特色，不可替代。重视民族典籍的翻译和研究工作，对于挖掘各民族优秀文化，保护各民族文明，增强各民族之间的沟通和了解，进一步向世界其他地区传播各少数民族优秀文化，乃至提高我国文化软实力都有着重要意义。不少少数民族聚居地处于祖国边疆，有的处在"一带一路"建设关键部位，有的处在与周边国家进行各种交流的重要位置。

　　中国民族典籍是世界多元文化的有机组成部分，与其他文化共同造就了世界文化的绚丽多姿。世界正因为其文化多样性才变得缤纷多彩。我国各民族典籍中包含的文化多样性极大地丰富了世界多元、特色鲜明的文化。人们对多样性形成全新的认识角度和思维方式。多样性开阔了人们的视野，丰富了人们思考问题的角度。挖掘这些典籍中所蕴含的教育价值和文化价值，对世界其他民族都有指导和借鉴意义，并且有助于建设我国的文化自信。

民族典籍本身蕴含的特殊价值对加强民族文化了解、促进中外文化交流具有重大意义。民族典籍英译具有文学翻译和文化传递之功能，有对外宣传作用，还是一种文学外交。因此，民族典籍翻译和研究对于维护祖国统一、促进民族团结、稳定边疆以及增强国内各民族和中外文化之间的交流都起着极为重要的作用。

中华人民共和国成立以后，中央政府一直十分重视民族典籍翻译和研究工作，提供了强有力的政策支持，并采取了一系列有效措施，加快了各少数民族典籍的抢救、整理、翻译和研究的进程。中央政府多次召开西藏工作会议和新疆工作会议。近年来，国际和国内对于多元文化高度关注，少数民族文学典籍的翻译已然成为业内研究的热点。

近年来，民族典籍翻译和研究迅猛发展，势头良好。国家大力支持，发放国家社科基金课题，教育部和国家民委也发放课题，扶持了一大批研究者。很多民族典籍翻译课题得以立项并顺利开展；为数不少的民族典籍被翻译成汉语、英语和其他语言并出版发行；越来越多的业界人士致力于这个满富生机的学术领域。

在中国文化走出去的国家战略下，全国少数民族典籍英译学术研讨会陆续召开，已经召开三次。

云南是中国民族最多的省份。人口在 5000 人以上的少数民族有 25 个，其中有 15 个民族为云南所特有，分别是：白族、哈尼族、傣族、傈僳族、佤族、拉祜族、纳西族、景颇族、布朗族、普米族、阿昌族、基诺族、怒族、德昂族、独龙族。其中除白族人口占全国白族人口总数的 84% 以上外，其他 14 个民族 95% 居住在云南。

云南还是我国跨境民族最多的省份。在云南的 25 个少数民族中，有 16 个民族跨境而居，分别是：傣族、壮族、苗族、景颇族、瑶族、哈尼族、德昂族、佤族、拉祜族、彝族、阿昌族、傈僳族、布依族、怒族、布朗族、独龙族。

云南少数民族创造了辉煌的文化。据不完全统计，云南少数民族文字文献古籍蕴藏量达 10 万余册（卷），口传古籍 4 万余种。云南省民委少数民族古籍整理出版规划办公室为了挽救和保护这些古籍，计划在 5 年内编纂出版 100 卷《云南少数民族古籍珍本集成》。这是一个令人瞩目的庞大计划。将这些古籍中的珍品翻译介绍给世界，不仅能够弘扬云南省丰富多彩的民族文化，而且有助于增进与南亚东南亚国家的理解与交流，为"一带一路"倡议的实施做出贡献。

云南师范大学外国语学院很重视这一领域的工作。在外国语学院领导支持下，李昌银教授带领一个由教授和中青年学者组成的团队对精选出来的 17 部云南少数民族经典作品进行英译，计划在 5 年内（"十三五"期间）翻译出版。这是一项十分有意义的宏大工程。

这 17 部民族典籍，内容全部为各民族的英雄史诗或神话传说，具有很高的历史意义和文学价值。这些作品涉及阿昌族、白族、傣族、德昂族、哈尼族、景颇族、拉祜族、苗族、纳西族、普米族、彝族等11个少数民族。

云南师范大学这支翻译队伍实力强大，主要由一些多年从事翻译教学、研究和实践的教授和副教授组成，他们是李昌银、黄瑛、彭庆华、孙兴文、吴相如、刘德周、杨慧芳、郜菊、陈萍、包琼（Joan Boulerice）等国内外专家学者。他们在云南翻译界都是风云人物。

在民族典籍英译中，这支队伍异军突起，为我国民族典籍英译壮大了声势，必将为中国民族典籍走向世界而成为世界文学的一部分做出新贡献。

民族典籍翻译与研究事业关乎国家的稳定统一，关乎民族关系的和谐发展，关乎世界多元文化的实现。在中国，民族典籍资源极为丰富，有待进一步挖掘、翻译。因此，民族典籍英译前景光明。同时，我们也应意识到，仍有许多濒临消失的少数民族典籍亟待拯救，民族典籍翻译与研究工作任重而道远。

（李正栓，中国英汉语比较研究会典籍英译专业委员会常务副会长兼秘书长）

Foreword by Li Zhengshuan

The translation of Chinese ethnic classics is an important approach in spreading Chinese culture, literature and civilization. It is a crucial component of Chinese culture going global. The spreading of Chinese culture and literature is a national policy and an important way to improve the cultural soft power of China. It plays an indispensable role in the cultural exchange between China and other countries and the development of world literature.

The ethnic groups in China have countless excellent classics with high anthropological, literary and cultural value. The ancestors of each ethnic group have passed down their distinctive culture orally or in writing. Almost all the ethnic groups have their own story of creation, epics, myths and legends.

Chinese ethnic classics are unique and irreplaceable. It is imperative to attach importance to the translation and research of ethnic classics; to explore the excellent ethnic cultures; to protect the civilization of ethnic groups; to enhance the communication and understanding among ethnic groups; to further spread the outstanding culture of ethnic groups to other parts of the world; and to build the cultural strength of China. Many ethnic groups live in the border areas and thus play an important role in the cultural and economic cooperation between China and its neighbors in the context of the Belt and Road Initiative.

Chinese ethnic classics are an important component of the magnificence and diversity of world culture. It is diversity that makes the world so colorful. The cultural diversity of Chinese ethnic classics has greatly enriched the world's pluralism and its distinctive features. People around the world have formed a new understanding of diversity. This diversity has expanded people's horizon and enriched their way of thinking. Digging out the educational and cultural value in these classics can contribute to the construction of China's self-confidence in culture.

The special value of the ethnic classics itself is of great significance to the strengthening of national culture and intercultural communication between China and foreign countries. The translation of ethnic classics is not just a literary exchange, but also a form of cultural communication. It is diplomacy through literature in that it consolidates the cultural ties between China and other countries.

After the founding of the People's Republic of China, the central government attached great importance to the translation and research of ethnic classics, provided the a great deal of policy support, and adopted a series of effective measures to speed up the process of rescuing, collating, translating and studying ethnic classics. The central government has convened several working conferences on Tibet and Xinjiang. In recent years, both China and other countries have paid close attention to multiculture. The translation of ethnic classics has become a hot topic.

In recent years, the translation and research of ethnic classics have progressed rapidly and have shown good prospects. The government strongly supports and grants the research projects of the national social science fund. The Ministry of Education and the State Ethnic Affairs Commission are also issuing research projects and giving funding to a large number of researchers. Many research projects on ethnic classics have been approved and carried out. Many ethnic classics have been translated into Chinese, English and other languages and published. More and more professionals have dedicated themselves to this new sphere of learning.

In this context, the academic conferences on translation of ethnic classics are held one after another all around the country. And up to now three have been held.

Yunnan is the province which has the most ethnic groups in China. Besides Han people, there are 25 ethnic groups, each with a population of more than 5,000. Among them, 15 ethnic groups are unique to Yunnan, which are the Bai, the Hani, the Dai, the Lisu, the Wa, the Lahu, the Naxi, the Jingpo, the Bulang, the Pumi, the Achang, the Jinuo, the Nu, the De'ang and the Dulong. Among these, 84% of the total number of the Bai people in China and 95% of the other 14 ethnic groups are living in Yunnan.

Yunnan is also the province which has the most cross-border ethnic groups. Of the 25 ethnic groups, 16 live across the border, namely: the Dai, the Zhuang, the Miao, the Jingpo, the Yao, the Hani, the De'ang, the Wa, the Lahu, the Yi, the Achang, the Lisu, the Buyi, the Nu, the Bulang and the Dulong.

The ethnic groups in Yunnan have created splendid cultures. According to statistics, the number of classics of Yunnan ethnic groups is more than 100 thousand volumes and classics in oral tradition are more than 40 thousand. In order to save and protect these ancient books, the Office of Classics Collation and Publishing of Yunnan Ethnic Groups Affairs Commission planned to compile and publish 100 volumes of *A Collection of Yunnan Ethnic Group Rare Books* in five years, which is an ambitious plan. The introduction of the ancient classics via translation can not only promote and develop the colorful ethnic cultures of Yunnan, but also contribute to the understanding and exchange between China and countries in South Asia and Southeast Asia and to the implementation of the Belt and Road Initiative as well.

The School of Foreign Languages and Literature of Yunnan Normal University is paying close attention to this field. With the support of the School and the University, Professor Li Changyin is leading a group of professors and young scholars to do the project of *"Classics of Yunnan Ethnic Groups in English Translation"*, which includes 17 ethnic classics selected carefully from Yunnan's bountiful ethnic classics. These books are the heroic epics or myths and legends of each ethnic groups with great historical significance and literary value. They will finish the translation in five years (during "the thirteenth five-year plan"). After that, all the works will be published by Yunnan People's Publishing House.

The 17 works cover 11 ethnic groups: the Achang, the Bai, the Dai, the De'ang, the Hani, the Jingpo, the Lahu, the Miao, the Naxi, the Pumi and the Yi. All of these groups except the Miao and the Yi are unique to Yunnan.

The translation team of Yunnan Normal University is full of strength and vitality, composed of professors and associate professors who have been occupied in translation teaching, research, and practice for a long time. They are Li Changyin, Huang Ying, Peng Qinghua, Sun Xingwen, Wu Xiangru, Liu Dezhou, Yang Huifang, Gao Ju, Chen Ping, Joan Boulerice and other experts and scholars who are representative figures in the translation field in Yunnan province.

This team is a new force that has suddenly arisen in terms of translating ethnic classics. It is expanding the momentum of ethnic classics translation in China and has made a new contribution for China's ethnic classics to go global and become a part of world literature.

The translation and research of ethnic classics are related

to the development of Chinese culture and the realization of multiculturalism in the world. In China, ethnic classics are extremely rich in resources, which require us to make further exploration and research and translate them into other languages. Therefore, the future of translating ethnic classics is bright. At the same time, we should also realize that there are still many ethnic works which are close to extinction and urgently need to be rescued. We still have a long way to go in the fields of translation and research in ethnic classics.

(Li Zhengshuan, Standing Vice Chairman and Secretary General, Classics Translation Committee of CACSEC)

序 二

◎王 宏

好友云南师范大学外国语学院李昌银教授来电嘱托我为"云南少数民族经典作品英译文库"的出版写一序言，并随即发来该文库的背景资料，让我"不着急，慢慢写"。我本人从事中国典籍英译及研究，深知少数民族典籍对外传译的重要性，但又是少数民族典籍翻译的门外汉。因此，我是怀着虚心学习的态度来写此序言的。近年来，在中国文化"走出去"战略工程大背景下，在中央和地方各级政府的大力支持下，我国少数民族典籍的对外传译及研究工作顺利开展，取得了很大的进步。请看以下数据：

2008年，广西百色学院韩家权教授获批国家社科基金项目《布洛陀史诗》（壮汉英对照）。该项目已顺利结项，并于2013年12月获得中国民间文艺最高奖"山花奖"。

2012年，广西百色学院外语系翻译团队翻译的国家级非物质文化遗产《壮族嘹歌》（英文版）由广西师范大学出版社正式出版。

2012年，东北大学秦皇岛分校吴松林教授主编的《蒙古族系列：江格尔（汉英对照）》（上下册）由吉林大学出版社出版。

2013年，河北师范大学李正栓教授英译《藏族格言诗》

由长春出版社出版发行。

2013年，云南财经大学崔晓霞教授撰写的《〈阿诗玛〉英译研究》收入由王宏印教授主编、民族出版社出版的"民族典籍翻译研究丛书"。

2014年，东北大学秦皇岛分校吴松林教授撰写的《满族档案文献研究》申请到国家社科后期资助，他英译的《英雄格斯尔可汗》由吉林大学出版社出版。

2014年，中南民族大学张立玉教授主持的"土家族主要典籍英译及研究"获批国家社科基金项目。

2015年，西安外国语大学梁真惠副教授撰写的《〈玛纳斯〉翻译传播研究》收入由王宏印教授主编、民族出版社出版的"民族典籍翻译研究丛书"。

与此同时，第一届和第二届全国少数民族典籍英译学术研讨会分别于2012年和2014年在广西民族大学和大连民族学院举行，参加会议的院校分布之广、与会代表数量之众、提交论文数量之多和涉及研究话题之细，十分可喜。2016年还将在中南民族大学举行第三届全国少数民族典籍英译学术研讨会。

为什么少数民族典籍的对外传译及研究工作在短短几年就受到译界的青睐，取得众多成果？我认为，这在很大程度上归于典籍翻译界乃至翻译界同仁对"中国典籍"的重新思考和认识。中国典籍浩如烟海，卷帙浩繁，举世瞩目，是全人类共同的精神财富。但对于中国典籍的理解，我们以前较多限于汉民族的重要文献和书籍，而对少数民族多有忽略。在讨论中国典籍时，也较多关注古代文学作品。其实，中国典籍指"中国清代末年1911年以前的重要文献和书籍",这就要求我们从事典籍翻译时,不但要翻译古代文学典籍作品,还要翻译古代哲学、科技、法律、医学、经济、军事、天文、地理等诸多方面的典籍作品,不但要翻译汉民族的典籍作品,也要翻译各少数民族的典籍作品。

民族典籍具有该民族的原型符号的特质,蕴藏着能够"遗传"并不断"再生"的文化基因。民族典籍是中华传统文化的内核,同时还是中华传统文化的符号构成规则。中国是具有56个民族的多民族国家,少数民族典籍是我国少数民族勤劳与智慧的结晶,是中华文明、也是世界文明不可或缺的一部分。少数民族典籍对外传译具有跨文化交流的作用,它不但有助于更多的人了解少数民族的独特文化,而且还有助于保护少数民族文化的独特性、维持少数民族文化多样性、促进各民族团结、提升中华文化软实力等。

中国少数民族典籍涉及宗教、文学、历史、语言、医学、天文历算等领域,内容丰富,版本多样,载体特殊,传承奇特。仅以《中国少数民族古籍总目提要》为例,该书于1997年正式立项,全书总体设计约60卷、110册,目前已出版23个民族卷共20册:纳西族卷、白族卷、东乡族卷·裕固族卷·保安族卷、土族卷·撒拉族卷、锡伯族卷、哈尼族卷、回族卷·铭刻、柯尔克孜族卷、羌族卷、毛南族卷·京族卷、仫佬族卷、达斡尔族卷、土家族卷、鄂温克族卷、鄂伦春族卷、赫哲族卷、苗族卷、侗族卷、黎族卷、朝鲜族卷。该书真实地反映了我国各少数民族古籍赋存的全面情况,充实了中国的历史和文化内容,为后人探索各种文化形式的源流、揭示中国社会文化发展的轨迹提供了极为珍贵的资料,为我国乃至世界各国人文科学研究提供了一套新颖而全面的资料,对于弘扬中华民族传统文化具有深远的历史意义和现实意义。

少数民族典籍的对外传译是一项艰巨的工作,涉及将少数民族语言译成汉语、少数民族语言之间的互译和少数民族语言译成外语(主要是英语)。前两类翻译历史源远流长,最早可追溯到春秋战国时代《越人歌》的翻译,即汉、壮语之间的翻译。少数民族典籍译成外语的时间则要晚一些。据考证,维吾尔族古典长诗《福乐智慧》成书于1069年或1070年,目前尚未发现完整的原稿,只存留下来三个抄本,分别为赫拉特抄本、费尔干纳抄本与埃及抄本,其中费尔干纳抄本于12~13世纪用阿拉伯文纳斯赫体抄写,1914年发现于今中亚乌孜别克斯坦纳曼干城,现存于该共和国科学院东方研究所。这是少数民族典籍译介到国外的最早纪录。少数民族典籍外译在现代有了较快发展。一些少数民族典籍,如藏族的《格萨尔王传》、蒙古族的《江格尔》和柯尔克孜族的《玛纳斯》等英雄史诗,云南彝族的《阿诗玛》、维吾尔族的《艾里甫和赛乃姆》等民间叙事长诗已先后被翻译成英语及其他外国文字,为世人所知。这对传承少数民族经典,推动中外文化交流起到了不可替代的作用。然而,还有大量的中国少数民族典籍等待我们去翻译和研究。

云南省少数民族典籍资源十分丰富。据不完全统计,云南少数民族文字文献古籍蕴藏量达10万余册(卷),口传古籍4万余种。"云南少数民族经典作品英译文库"正是依托云南省丰富的少数民族典籍资源,借助云南师范大学外国语学院强大的翻译师资队伍，在云南人民出版社的有力支持下，首次将云南少数民族经典作品成系列对外译介的大力举措。云南师范大学外国语学院对"云南少数民族经典作品英译文库"十分重视，他们首先邀请省内外少数民族语言文化研究专家对云南民族典籍和民族文化经典作品进行筛选，做到"好中选好，优中选优"，同时调配最强的翻译力量承担文库的翻译任务。我粗略看了该文库的选题，发现选题面广，覆盖范围宽，收入了云南省阿昌族、白族、傣族、纳西族、德昂族、哈尼族、景颇族、拉祜族、苗族、普米族和彝族等民族的典籍作品。云南共有25个少数民族，其中11个少数民族的典籍作品都覆盖到了，不少作品还是首次译成英文。这将彻底改变云南少数民族典籍由于对外译介数量较少，不为世界了解的尴尬局面。

对于云南师范大学外国语学院而言，把少数民族典籍英译作为翻译专业的优势特色进行建设，这将对该院的学科建设起到助推作用。"云南少数民族经典作品英译文库"所产生的翻译成果和研究成果将培养出一批优秀的典籍翻译和研究团队，凸显该院在全国的学术特色和学术影响，同时还能将翻译能力和研究能力转化为教学能力，提高云南师范大学外国语学院翻译专业研究生的培养质量，为社会输送高水平的翻译人才，有力地支撑学院翻译专业学科的建设和发展。我对云南师范大学外国语学院的翻译师资队伍较为熟悉。作为云南省唯一获得省级高校优势特色学科建设项目的外国语学院，该院具有雄厚的翻译师资力量，在云南省各高校中当属第一。多年来，该院翻译与跨文化研究团队一直承担着对外交流与合作的各种口笔译项目及任务。由外国语学院精心挑选和确定的"云南少数民族经典作品英译文库"翻译人员绝大多数都是云南省翻译领域里的知名教授或专家，有国外留学经历，且具有扎实的英汉双语语言功底，曾翻译出版多部译著和翻译作品，并且主持和参与过多项翻译项目的研究。我阅读李昌银教授发来的文库翻译人员名单，发现多名我所熟悉的知名教授、博士也在其中，感到格外放心。

"云南少数民族经典作品英译文库"的出版发行是云南省翻译界的一件大事，也是我国少数民族典籍翻译传来的又一佳音。想当年，我和《大中华文库》总协调人李林老师曾在参加全国典籍英译学术研讨会之余一起找到李昌银教授，敦促李教授向学校和同事呼吁，少数民族典籍翻译及研究是富矿，值得快挖、深挖，能早出成果，出大成果。今天，我们当年的心愿变成了美好的现实，心里感到特别高兴。再次热烈祝贺"云南少数民族经典作品英译文库"的顺利出版！

（王宏，中国典籍翻译研究会副会长、苏州大学博士生导师）

Foreword by Wang Hong

My friend Professor Li Changyin of Yunnan Normal University asked me to write a few words for the publication of *Classics of Yunnan Ethnic Groups in English Translation*. I am more than delighted to do it. As I have been doing research in the English translation of Chinese classics, I know how important his work is. In recent years, substantial progress has been made in translating Chinese ethnic classics into English and other foreign languages. Books published in this respect include *The Liao Songs of the Zhuang Nationality* (Nanning: Guangxi Normal University Press, 2008, English Edition), *Mongolian Series: Jianggeer* (Changchun: Jilin University Press, 2012, Bilingual Edition), *Tibetan Gnomic Verses Translated into English* (Changchun: Changchun Press, 2013), and *Geser Khan: a Hero* (Changchun: Jilin University Press, 2014). Several projects in the English translation of ethnic classics have received funding from the National Planning Office of Philosophy and Social Science and, as a result, a number of monographs and PhD dissertations have been published.

Meanwhile, it is encouraging to see that the first conferences on English translation of ethnic classics in China have been held in Guangxi Nationalities University and

Dalian Nationalities Institute respectively. Participants were both many and enthusiastic. Many papers were presented and a lot of topics discussed. The third conference will be hosted by South Central Nationalities University in 2016.

Why, then, has this field attracted so much attention from translators and scholars alike and accomplished so much in just a few years? The answer, I believe, lies in a rethinking of what constitutes Chinese classics as an indispensable part of human heritage. We used to see Chinese classics as more or less equal to the classics of the Han people, excluding works by other ethnic groups. Moreover, when we talk about Chinese classics, we focus too much on the literary works of ancient times. Yet Chinese classics actually refer to "important works and books before 1911, the year when the Qing dynasty fell, bringing an end to imperial rule." This definition requires us to pay attention not just to literary works, but also writings in other subjects, such as philosophy, science, law, medicine, economics, military affairs, astronomy, and geography, not only Han works, but writings by other ethnic groups as well.

The classical works of a nation are its archetypal symbols, the major carriers of its cultural genes. Chinese classics make up the core of Chinese tradition. The Chinese nation consists of 56 ethnic groups. Ethnic classics are an important part of not only Chinese traditional culture, but also of world civilization. The translation of these works into other languages is important in that it helps to promote cross-cultural communications between China and other countries and to protect and preserve the uniqueness and diversity of ethnic cultures by making them accessible to foreign readers.

Chinese ethnic classics cover a variety of areas, such as religion, literature, history, language, medicine, astrology, and calendar, with numerous editions, special media and unique ways of transmission from generation to generation. Take, for example, *An Anthology of Chinese Ethnic Classics*, a colossal project that includes 110 volumes, 20 of which, from 23 ethnic groups, have been published. The anthology reflects the variety and quantity of China's ethnic classics and provides valuable material and resources for studying, understanding and developing Chinese culture and history in a more comprehensive and sustainable way.

The translation of Chinese ethnic classics into foreign languages is a very demanding job, involving rendering from ethnic languages to Chinese, between ethnic languages, and from ethnic languages (often via Chinese) to foreign languages. The first two types of translation can be traced back to the Spring and Autumn Period, when *The Song of the Yue People* was translated from their mother tongue into Chinese. The earliest translation of ethnic classics into a foreign language is *Wisdom of Royal Glory*, a long poem of the Uygurs, which was rendered from the source language into Arabic and is now in the Oriental Institute of Uzbekistan at Namangan. But it was not until modern times that the translation of ethnic classics into foreign languages accelerated. Noticeably, ethnic epics, such as *The Story of Prince Geser* of the Tibetans, *The Story of Jianggeer* of the Mongolians, *Manas* of the Kyrgyz, and narrative poems such as *Ashima* of the Yi people, *Alip and Salam* of the Uygurs, etc., have been published. These translations have contributed to acquainting the world with Chinese ethnic classics, but many remain to be translated.

Yunnan is rich in ethnic classics, boasting more than 100 thousand volumes of written classics and over 40 thousand pieces of oral literature. Relying on such bountiful resources, as a collective endeavor of the translation team of the School of Foreign Languages and Literature, Yunnan Normal University and with the help of Yunnan People's Publishing House, *Classics of Yunnan Ethnic Groups in English Translation* is the first project to translate Yunnan ethnic classics into English on a large scale. The School adheres to a professional spirit and academic standard in carrying out the project by selecting the most authoritative texts in the source language (Chinese) and recruiting the best translators from its huge faculty. The selection of the works, covering eleven of the twenty-five ethnic groups of the province, indicates expertise and insight. The implementation of the project will change the embarrassing obscurity of Yunnan ethnic classics by making them known to the world, many of them for the first time.

In light of disciplinary development, the project is of

great importance, too. Participating in the translation will strengthen the academic foundation of the teachers, enrich their experience and enhance their translation skills and research ability. This in turn will help them become better teachers and thus able to educate students with higher quality. The publication of the books will add greatly to the faculty accomplishments of the School and raise the academic standing of Yunnan Normal University by taking the first step in this direction among the universities of Yunnan province.

This publication project is a great event not only for Yunnan itself, but also for China. Looking back, I remember that Professor Li Changyin, our friend Li Lin, editor of the *Library of Chinese Classics*, and I talked enthusiastically about initiating something like this in Yunnan when we attended a conference on the translation of ethnic classics in Soochow. Lin and I strongly suggested that Professor Li do it as soon as possible. Now I am very pleased to see our talk becoming reality. Again, my congratulations on the publication of *Classics of Yunnan Ethnic Groups in English Translation*!

(Wang Hong, PhD supervisor at Soochow University, Vice Chairman of Classics Translation Committee of CACSEC)

查姆// Chamu

General Introduction

This publication project, Classics of *Yunnan Ethnic Groups in English Translation*, aims at introducing Yunnan ethnic classical works to the world by making them available to native speakers of English who might be interested in them. With the publication of the *Library of Chinese Classics*, which consists only of books written by Han authors in classical Chinese, attention now is being turned to the English translation and publication of ethnic classics, books produced by ethnic writers about their history and culture. Universities in provinces such as Guangxi, Guizhou, Liaoning, Xinjiang, and Xizang, have taken the initiative. We in Yunnan must do something, because Yunnan has the largest number of ethnic groups in China. 15 of the 25 ethnic groups in the province, the Bai, the Dai, the Hani, the Lisu, the Wa, the Lahu, the Naxi, the Jingpo, the Bulang, the Pumi, the Achang, the Jinuo, the Nu, the De'ang, and the Dulong, live in no other place but Yunnan. The classics of these people, either in their own languages or in Chinese translations, are a great treasure house, which should be accessible to English readers and scholars. But what works should be translated first?

All the 25 ethnic groups in Yunnan have their classics, epics, mythology, creation stories, folksongs, folk drama, mountain songs, and funeral lament lyrics, most of which exist in different versions in different places. According to one estimation, there are more than 100 thousand volumes of them, excluding those in oral form. After a thorough survey and extensive consultations with experts of ethnic studies, we concluded that priority must be given to epics and mythologies, as they reflect an ethnic people's philosophy, history and culture more than anything else by narrating the stories of where and how they think they came from. From many epics and mythologies, we selected 17 of the most authoritative and popular classics representing 11 Yunnan ethnic groups, the Yi, the Bai, the Miao, the Hani, the Lahu, the Naxi, the Jingpo, the Pumi, the Achang, the Dai, and the De'ang. These works are all in Chinese, translated from the original by bilingual scholars whose mother tongue is their own ethnic language and who are fluent and proficient in Chinese. Some were recorded from their oral form at rituals and performances. We did not choose texts written in the ethnic language, not least because it is very hard to find a translator who is skilled in both the ethnic language and English. Moreover, some of the classics in the ethnic language were circulated in various oral forms and fragments. The published Chinese versions have been carefully edited and translated, hence they are more reliable. The next question is: how to translate them?

It happens that all of the 17 works except one are in

verse form, with lines more or less the same length and loose rhymes, but no regular meter. A poem must be rendered into a poem; anything less is unacceptable. So here are the general rules we follow when doing the translation.

One. If the original is verse, the translated text must be verse, too.

Two. Reproduce the ideas and the images of the original as completely as possible.

Three. Reproduce the figures of speech of the original as much as possible.

Four. Do not change the number of lines in a stanza unless absolutely necessary.

Five. Do not use standard meters in English, because the Chinese original does not follow any regular meter. Use the natural rhythm of English instead, but most of the lines should look more or less the same length.

Six. Do not use rhyme unless it comes naturally and is faithful to the content of the original.

What we try to do is, to use Susan Bassnett's words, "transplant the seed", not the tree itself. As for the various aspects of form, particularly meter and end rhyme, we reproduce them when it is possible and abandon them when it is necessary.

Who will do the translations? As this is a collective project of the School of Foreign Languages and Literature of Yunnan Normal University, our team consists of a dozen faculty members and two students from our MA translation program who are already teachers in other universities. All the translators have been teaching translation and doing translation research for a long time. They have published not just academic articles on translation, but also translated books from English to Chinese or vice versa.

Traditionally, people translate into their mother tongue, not into a foreign language. But the situation is changing. Many translators today are translating from their mother tongue into a foreign language. The quality can be good, as Nike K. Pokorn and Stuart Campbell prove in *Challenging the Traditional Axioms*: *Translation into a non-mother tongue* (Amsterdam: John Benjamins Publishing Company, 2005) and *Translation into the Second Language* (New York: Routledge, 2013) respectively. The case of China provides further evidence for their argument. The translation of Chinese classics into English was initiated by James Legge and Herbert Allen Giles in the 19th century and carried on in the 20th century by Arthur Waley, David Hawkes, Burton Watson, John Minford, Stephen Owen and others. It is noticeable that these English and American sinologists were soon joined by Chinese scholars residing in the West, such as Hongming (Tomson) Gu and Lin Yutang, among others. They took up the job because they thought it was their obligation to give English readers more faithful translations than Western sinologists could, who, as their target language is their mother tongue, often misinterpret the original text and misrepresent Chinese culture. Since the 1950s, there has been an increasingly powerful trend for Mainland Chinese translators to render or re-render Chinese classics into foreign languages, English in particular. In our time, this work is gathering momentum, enthusiastically advocated and actively practiced by such well-known translation experts as Yang Xianyi of Beijing Foreign Language Press, Xu Yuanchong of Beijing University, Wang Rongpei of Dalian Foreign Language Institute, Wang Hongyin of Nankai University, Wang Hong of Soochow University, Li Zhengshuan of Hebei Normal University, and many more. These professors are not just translators, but also scholars in translation studies. More importantly, some of them, Xu Yuanchong, Wang Hong and Li Zhengshuan, for example, have had their translations published by Western publishers, which suggests that their English meets the international standard.

In the case of our project, we request that the translators do their best to produce good translations. When they submit them to us, they should represent the highest level that they can attain. Then the general editors appointed by the School read the translated texts and remove inaccurate renderings and grammar mistakes if there are any. On top of that, we've taken an indispensable measure to ensure that our English is readable. We asked Ms. Joan Cecile Boulerice, an American teacher who has been teaching English in our school since

2009, to read every text that we've translated and improve the English by making it more natural and idiomatic. This is the best we can do. Of course any problems that still remain in the translations are ours. They have nothing to do with our American teacher.

As the project is well under way, we would like to thank all those who have helped to make it possible. Ms Guo Muyu, director of the South and Southeast Asia Editorial Department, Yunnan People's Publishing House, has been most helpful in our cooperation. In addition, she has added importance to the project by turning it into a national publication project. Yunnan Normal University has supported us by paying the publication fees so that the translators won't have to be burdened with the financial responsibilities for this project. Professor Li Zhengshuan and Professor Wang Hong not only have always encouraged us to go on but have also written the forewords for the project, putting it in a global perspective. Ms Joan Boulerice's revision has ensured the fluency of the translated texts. Finally, special thanks must be given to Professor Wang Hong, again, and Mr Li Lin of Hunan People's Press for their suggestion that has helped us conceive the project from the very beginning.

(The General Editors, School of Foreign Languages & Literature, Yunnan Normal University, Kunming)

查姆 // Chamu

A Brief Introduction to *Chamu*

Chamu is the genesis epic of the Yi people. Among all the extant literature which reflect the lives and history of the Yi people during the primitive age, *Chamu* is a written work that ranks at the top in its length, popularity and influence. Cha means origin. Yi people define the narration for the origin of something on earth as a cha. Chamu means the origin of everything.

Chamu is regarded as the cultural root of the Yi people, the treasure house of Yi literature and the encyclopedia of the Yi people. *Chamu* covers many miraculous legends and touching myths that have been told by generations of Yi people. The main content includes the creation of the world, the flood, the origin of human beings, the origin of ethnic groups, the origin of everything and the elixir. All the myths recorded in *Chamu* are rooted in the lives of the Yi people during the primitive age. The epic is a product of human ideology in clan society. We can see a miniature of the primitive age through *Chamu*. We can see how humans fought the powerful force of nature to survive in very tough situations. We can hear the footsteps of human society evolving from low levels to higher ones. The achievements of the ancestors of the Yi people have contributed a lot to the progress of human society.

The Translators

查姆 | 目录

上　部 // 1

序　诗 // 2

第一章　天地的起源 // 6

第二章　独眼睛时代 // 28

第三章　直眼睛时代 // 60

第四章　横眼睛时代 // 110

下　部 // 155

第一章　麻和棉 // 156

第二章　绸和缎 // 178

第三章　金银铜铁锡 // 196

第四章　纸和笔 // 214

第五章　书 // 232

第六章　长生不老药 // 254

- 1 -

Contents

Book One // 1

Prologue // 3

Canto 1   The Creation of the World // 7

Canto 2   The One-Eyed Era // 29

Canto 3   The Vertical-Eyed Era // 61

Canto 4   The Horizontal-Eyed Generation // 111

Book Two // 155

Canto 1   Flax and Cotton // 157

Canto 2   Silk and Brocade // 179

Canto 3   Gold, Silver, Copper, Iron and Tin // 197

Canto 4   Paper and Brush Pen // 215

Canto 5   Books // 233

Canto 6   The Elixir // 255

上部
Book One

序　诗

人类最早那一代，
他们的名字叫"拉爹"①，
他们只有一只眼，
独眼生在脑门心。

"拉爹"下一代，
名字叫"拉拖"②，
他们有两只直眼睛，
两只直眼朝上生。

"拉拖"的后一代，
名字叫"拉文"③，
他们有两只横眼睛，
两眼平平朝前生。

---

① 拉爹：独眼睛那代人的名字。
② 拉拖：直眼睛那代人的名字。
③ 拉文：横眼睛那代人的名字。彝族先民把人类分为独眼睛、直眼睛、横眼睛三个时代。

Book One

Prologue

The first generation of human beings
Were called Ladie①.
They had only one eye
In the middle of the forehead.

The generation after Ladie
Were called Latuo②.
They had two vertical eyes
Standing on and side by side.

The generation after Latuo
Were called Lawen③.
They had two horizontal eyes
In the front of their head.

---

① Ladie: the name of the generation with only one eye.
② Latuo: the name of the generation with two vertical eyes.
③ Lawen: the name of the generation with two horizontal eyes. The ancestors of the Yi people divided human beings into three generations, known as one-eyed generation, two-vertical-eyed generation and two-horizontal-eyed generation respectively.

"拉文"是我们的祖先,
最早的"拉文"是两兄妹,
他俩名叫阿朴独姆①,
阿朴独姆西是他们的子孙。

亲亲的阿哥,
亲亲的阿姐,
请慢慢听彝家的"查"②,
请细细听彝家的古根。

---

① 阿朴独姆:阿朴独姆是两兄妹的共同名字。
② 查:起源。

Lawen is our ancestor,

The earliest Lawens were brother and sister,

They were named Apudumu①,

And their descendants were named Apudumuxi.

Dear brother,

Dear sister,

Please listen to the Cha② of the Yi people,

Please enjoy the genesis of the Yi people.

---

① Apudumu: the common name of the brother and sister.
② Cha: genesis, origin.

第一章 天地的起源

远古的时候,
天地连成一片。
下面没有地,
上面没有天,
分不出黑夜,
分不出白天。

只有雾露一团团,
只有雾露滚滚翻。
雾露里有地,
雾露里有天,
时昏时暗多变幻,
时清时浊年复年。

天翻成地,
地翻成天,
天地混沌分不清,
天地雾露难分辨。

上部
Book One

Canto 1　The Creation of the World

Long long ago,
The world was in chaos.
There was no earth below,
Nor sky above.
Night and day
Were not distinguished.

Every place was overwhelmed by the mist,
It billowed here and there.
The earth was faint in the mist;
The sky was faint in the mist.
Dim and dark they turned,
Brightness and mistiness alternated.

The sky turned into the earth,
And the earth into the sky.
It was hard to distinguish the sky from the earth,
The mist veiled them both.

查姆 // Chamu

空中不见飞禽,
地上不见人烟。

没有草木生长,
没有座座青山;
没有滔滔大海,
没有滚滚河川;
没有太阳照耀,
没有星斗满天;
没有月亮发光,
更没打雷扯闪。

涅侬俫佐颇,
是所有神仙之王。
他召集众人神仙:
仙王入黄炸当地,
水王罗塔纪,
龙王罗阿玛①,
天王和地王,
还有他们的儿女。
众人神聚一起,
共同来商议;
要安排日月星辰,

---

① 罗阿玛:全名叫涅侬阿玛,是众龙王之王。

Book One

There were neither birds flying,
Nor human beings moving.

There were neither woods growing,
Nor mountains towering;
There were neither seas billowing,
Nor rivers rushing;
There was neither radiant sunshine,
Nor starry sky;
There was neither moonlight glistening,
Nor thunder or lightning.

Nienongluozuopo
Was the King of the Immortals.
He convened all the gods:
Ruhuangzhadangdi, the Fairy King,
Luotaji, the Water Goddess,
Luo'ama[①], the Dragon Queen,
The King of Heaven and the King of Earth,
And their sons and daughters.
All the gods gathered,
And discussed how to arrange
The sun, the moon and the stars,

---

① Luo'ama: her full name is Nienongama. She is the queen of all dragons.

查姆 // Chamu

要铸就宇宙山川，
要造天造地。

派龙王罗阿玛，
去到太空中，
种活一棵娑罗树，
树生四枝杈，
一杈生四叶，
四匹叶上四朵花。
这棵娑罗树，
是树木的祖先。
白天不开花，
夜晚白花鲜。

派撒赛萨若埃①，
到一千重天上，
种棵娑罗树，
树生四枝杈，
一杈生四叶，
四匹叶上四朵花。
花开红嫣嫣，
万颗金针刺双眼。
树花白天开，

---

① 撒赛萨若埃：涅侬倮佐颇的长子。

Book One

To create the world, hills and rivers,
And to make the sky and the earth.

Luo'ama, the Dragon Queen,
Was sent into space,
Where she planted a sala tree,
On which four branches grew.
Each branch had four leaves,
And each leaf had one flower.
This sala tree
Was the ancestor of all trees.
It did not bloom during the day,
But produced white flowers at night.

Sasaisaruo'ai① was sent
To distant skies,
Where he planted a sala tree,
On which four branches grew.
Each branch had four leaves,
And each leaf had one flower.
The flowers blossomed in red,
Giving off golden rays.
The trees flowered in the day,

---
① Sasaisaruo'ai: the eldest son of Nienongluozuopo.

查姆 // Chamu

日日花开照人间。

白天、黑夜两朵花,
轮流开在太空间。
白天开花是太阳,
夜晚开花是月亮;
太阳开花月不明,
月亮开花星不闪;
两花轮流开,
两花难相见。
十年花不谢,
万载花鲜艳。

派涅侬撒萨歇①,
在太空撒上星辰。
抬头望星星,
数也数不完,
夜晚眨眼睛,
星光亮闪闪。

星王曾色锡,
笑在太空中。
打开风水门,

---

① 涅侬撒萨歇:涅侬倮佐颇的次子。

Book One

Lighting the world every day.

The two flowers of the day and the night
Bloomed in the universe in turn.
The flower of the day was the sun,
The flower of the night was the moon;
The sun shadowed the moon in daylight,
The moon veiled the stars at night;
The two flowers appeared in turn,
They rarely met each other.
They bloomed for years,
They glowed for ages.

Nienongsasaxie[①] was sent
To sprinkle stars in the sky.
There were so many of them,
You couldn't count them all.
They twinkled at night
Like blinking eyes.

Zengsexi, the King of the Stars,
Smiled in the heavens.
He opened the door of wind and water,

---
① Nienongsasaxie: the second son of Nienongluozuopo.

查姆 // Chamu

雾露缥缈太空间。
雾露里有地,
雾露里有天;
雾露变气育万物,
万物生长天地间。

只有日月星辰,
还无宇宙山川。
还要造山河,
还要造蓝天。

神仙之王涅侬倮佐颇,
开口来指点:
地要造成簸箕样,
天要造得篾帽圆。
篾帽、簸箕才合得拢,
篾帽、簸箕合成地和天。

造人之神的女儿涅滨矮①,
设法造河川。
造下洪波万顷的大海,
造下纵横的沟渠河川,
造下湖泊和清泉,

---

① 涅滨矮:是造人之神儿依得罗娃的女儿。

Book One

And the mist hung everywhere,

Hiding the earth,

Dimming the sky;

The mist nurtured everything

In the universe.

Now there were only the sun, the moon and the stars,

But no universe, mountains or rivers,

Which were yet to be created.

And blue sky must also be made.

Nienongluozuopo, the King of the Immortals,

Gave the order:

The earth must be round like a winnowing basket,

The sky must be round like a bamboo hat.

The winnowing basket and the bamboo hat fit fine,

Together they form the earth and the sky.

Niebin'ai[①], daughter of man's Creator,

Managed to create rivers and streams.

She made billowing seas,

Zigzagging waterways,

Crystal-clear lakes and springs,

---

① Niebin'ai: daughter of Eryideluowa, man's Creator.

造下绿水和深潭。

水王罗塔纪,
是水中神仙。
她用海水养鱼养虾,
鱼在海底游,
虾在水中翻;
她管绿水有方,
绿水四季长流,
绿水映澈蓝天。
她管水里的万物,
她管龙潭深渊;
她管地上的万物,
她管地上的粮棉。

龙王罗阿玛心最细,
星星走动能听见。
她到九重天上找种子,
种子长在月中间。
月里那棵娑罗树,
树上良种数不完;
奇花异草由人选,
树木药材任人拣,
树上藏有谷子、苞谷,

上部
Book One

And blue pools and deep ponds.

Luotaji, the Water Goddess,
Was in charge of water.
She nurtured fish and shrimp in the sea,
Fish swam at the bottom,
And shrimp played near the surface;
She took good care of the blue water,
So that it was always abundant
And forever mirrored the sky.
She was in charge of all water creatures,
Dragon pools and distant deeps;
She was in charge of everything on land,
Including crops and cotton.

Luo'ama, the Dragon Queen, was so careful,
She could hear stars tiptoe.
In the sky she sought for seeds,
And found them in the middle of the moon,
Where there was the sala tree,
On which grew innumerable choice seeds.
Rare flowers and grass were ready to be picked,
Trees and herbs were waiting to be plucked,
Grain and corn were hidden in the tree,

树上储存果木麻棉;
还有荞子、洋芋,
还有甘蔗蜜甜……
有种子才有万物,
有万物才有人烟;
有种子祖先才能生存,
有粮食人类才能繁衍。
罗阿玛呵,想得周到,
罗阿玛呵,想得最远。

涅侬倮佐颇,
开口又指点:
大地造成了平原,
大地并不美观,
地面要有盆地,
地面要有高山。
既要有雨露滋润,
又要有阳光送暖,
这样才能种粮食,
人类才能生存发展。

龙王罗阿玛呵,
按照涅侬倮佐颇的吩咐,
又来到广阔的平原。

Fruit, hemp and cotton were stored there;

There were buckwheat and potatoes,

As well as honey-sweet sugarcane…

Seeds are the source of everything on earth,

Which is the source of human beings.

Seeds ensured our ancestors' survival;

Grain helped the reproduction of mankind.

Oh, Luo'ama was the most considerate,

Oh, Luo'ama was the most far-sighted.

Nienongluozuopo

Gave more orders:

The land is too flat.

It's not beautiful.

There must be plains on the land,

There must be mountains too;

There must be nourishing rainfall

And warm sunshine for all,

So that grain can grow,

And humans can survive and thrive.

Luo'ama, the Dragon Queen,

Followed the orders of Nienongluozuopo.

She headed for the vast plain.

她撒下倾盆大雨,
冲出沟河山川,
冲成峻岭深箐,
冲出丘陵河滩。
大地冒清泉,
遍地流水潺潺。

日复一日,
年复一年,
天上太阳又不亮,
天上月亮又不明。
神仙之王涅侬倮佐颇,
找来水王罗塔纪,
还有罗塔纪姑娘,
共同来商议。

水王罗塔纪说:
"由于日月不干净,
白天黑夜才分不清。"
神仙之王派罗塔纪姑娘,
飞到九千台天上,
去洗月亮和太阳。

罗塔纪姑娘,

上部
Book One

She poured heavy rain

To scour out highlands and channels,

Steep mountains and deep valleys,

And hills and flood land.

Clear springs bubbled here and there,

Flowing water was everywhere.

Day in and day out,

Year in and year out,

The sun stopped shining,

The moon stopped glistening.

Nienongluozuopo, the King of the Immortals,

Called Luotaji, the Water Goddess,

And her daughter, Princess Luotaji, to his place

To discuss the matter.

Luotaji, the Water Goddess, said:

"The sun and the moon are not clean.

That's why day and night can't be divided."

Princess Luotaji was given the task:

She flew through nine thousand spheres

To wash the sun and the moon.

Princess Luotaji

去到撑天的三座山上，
挑来一挑蓝海水，
挑来一挑金海水，
挑来一挑绿海水，
去洗日月身上的灰尘。

罗塔纪姑娘，
洗完星星洗月亮，
洗罢月亮洗太阳。
星星洗得亮晶晶，
星星黑夜眨眼睛；
月亮洗得亮堂堂，
太阳洗得白生生，
太阳白天耀眼明。

罗塔纪姑娘，
洗干净了星星，
洗干净了月亮，
洗干净了太阳。
从此天地不混沌，
昼夜辨得清，
四季分得明。
瞧着日出日落，
就能分出早晚；

Went to the three mountains that held up the sky.

She brought blue seawater,

She brought golden seawater,

She brought green seawater,

And washed the sun and the moon.

Princess Luotaji

Washed the stars first, then the moon,

And finally the sun.

The stars resumed sparkling

And twinkling in the evening sky;

The moon resumed its brightness,

And the sun started shining again

In the daytime, dazzling to the eyes.

Princess Luotaji

Washed the stars clean,

Washed the moon clean,

And washed the sun clean.

The world was no longer in chaos,

Day and night were divided,

The four seasons followed one after another.

Dawn and dusk could be distinguished

By sunrise and sunset.

看着月出月落,
就能分出昼夜;
看着草木盛衰,
能知寒暑冷暖;
瞧着庄稼生长,
能分四季变幻。

日月怎样走动?
白天黑夜怎样循环?
白天太阳走,
夜晚月亮转;
还有满天星星,
跟着月亮眨眼。

太阳和月亮,
轮流转玉盘。
它们是天地的眼睛,
专给大地照明送温暖。
天一睁眼,
太阳就露笑脸;
天一闭眼,
月亮、星星笑作一团。

天地间的事,

Book One

Day and night could be told
By the moon's rise and fall.
Heat and cold could be felt
From plant's blooming and withering.
The four seasons could be felt
From the crops' growing.

How did the sun and the moon move?
How did day and night alternate?
The sun showed up in the daytime,
The moon turned up at nighttime;
The numerous stars in the sky
Twinkled in the moonlight.

The sun and the moon
Rotated the jade plate in turn.
They were the eyes of the sky and the earth,
Providing light and warmth for the world.
When the sky opened its eyes,
The sun started smiling;
When the sky closed its eyes,
The moon and stars started giggling.

Of the things in the world,

查姆 // Chamu

地动是第一。
地转到金海旁边,
太阳出来啦!
地转到蓝海旁边,
月亮出来啦!
地转到绿海旁边,
星星出来啦!

万物在动中生,
万物在动中演变。
不动嘛不生,
不生嘛不长,
这就是天地的起始,
这就是万物的来源。

彝家把这个时代,
叫作托得多查①,
汉家把这个时代,
叫作盘古开天地。

---

① 托得多查:音译。查,源也;托得多,天地的意思;托得多查,天地的起源之意。

Book One

The moving of the earth was the first.
When the earth rotated to the golden sea,
The sun showed up!
When the earth rotated to the blue sea,
The moon showed up!
When the earth rotated to the green sea,
The stars showed up!

Things were born in movement,
And in movement they evolved.
Without movement, there was no birth,
Without birth, there was no growth.
This was the beginning of the world,
This was the origin of everything.

The Yi people call this era
Tuodeduocha[①],
The Han people call this period
Pangu's Creation of the world.

[①] Tuodeduocha: transliteration of the Yi words. Cha means origin and tuodeduo means the world. Together they mean the origin of the world.

第二章 独眼睛时代

有了日月星辰,

有了宇宙山川,

不能没有人烟;

有了江河湖泊,

有了种了粮棉,

不能没有人生活在天地间。

雾露缥缈大地,

变成绿水一潭。

水中有个姑娘,

名叫赛依列①,

她说"要造独眼睛时代的人",

就叫儿依得罗娃最先来造人。

儿依得罗娃,

造出人类的第一代祖先②,

---

① 赛依列:龙王的姑娘。
② 儿依得罗娃造人之说,原传说中还有两种说法:一种是她"塑起了两个人,男的那个眼睛有八只,耳朵有九只;女的那个手有四只,脚有两只……他们的眼睛不眨"。另一种说法是,她"塑了两个人,男人塑了八只眼,八只眼睛看万山;耳朵塑了九只,九只耳朵听得远;还塑了一支特殊眼,眼睛不眨看得宽。女人捏了六只手,六只巧手能胜天;女人捏成六只脚,六脚走得快"。这些传说有一定的参考价值,特注录于此。

上部
Book One

Canto 2 The One-Eyed Era

Now the sun, the moon and the stars were created,
The universe, mountains and rivers were shaped,
Human beings were needed;
Now rivers and lakes were made,
Seeds, crops and cotton were planted,
There should be human beings in the world.

The mist covered the land,
And turned into a green pond.
A girl stood in the water,
Her name was Saiyilie[①].
She said: "I want to create one-eyed human beings."
Eryideluowa was summoned to create human beings.
Eryideluowa created
The first generation of human beings,[②]

[①] Saiyilie: daughter of the Dragon Queen.
[②] The story that Eryideluowa created human beings has two versions. One version is that she "created a man and a woman. The man had eight eyes and nine ears while the woman had four hands and two legs... They don't blink their eyes." The other version is that she "created a man and a woman. The man had eight eyes which could detect things far away and nine ears which could hear even the faintest sound. He had a special eye which didn't blink and could see widely. The woman had six nimble hands and six swift feet."

他们的名字叫"拉爹"。
他们是天地的儿女,
他们是太阳的儿女,
他们是月亮的儿女,
他们是星星的儿女。
这代人只有一只眼,
独只眼睛长在哪里?
独只眼生在脑门心。

独眼睛这代人,
不会说话,
不会种田,
像野兽一样过光阴。
今天跟老虎打架,
明天和豹子硬拼;
人吃野兽,
野兽也吃人。
常常互相争斗,
有时还会人吃人。

独眼睛这代人,
深山老林作房屋,
野岭岩洞常栖身。
石头作工具,

Book One

Who were called Ladie.

They were children of the sky and the earth,

They were children of the sun,

They were children of the moon,

They were children of the stars.

They had only one eye,

Where was their eye located?

In the middle of the forehead.

The one-eyed generation

Could not speak,

Nor could they farm.

They led a beast-like life.

Sometimes they fought with tigers,

Sometimes they scuffled with leopards.

People ate beasts,

Beasts also ate people.

Men often fought with each other,

And even ate each other.

The one-eyed human beings

Hid in forests

And sheltered in caves and wilderness.

They used stones as tools

木棒当武器,
在风雨雷电中穿行。

独眼睛这代人,
树叶作衣裳,
乱草当被盖,
渴了喝凉水,
饿了吃野果,
草根树皮来充饥。
他们不知酸甜味,
他们苦辣不能分。

独眼睛这代人啊,
困了树下睡,
病了树下哼。
高兴拉着树枝跳,
有时狂叫有时笑,
在哭笑中生存。

独眼睛这代人啊,
慢慢认识野兽习性:
力大不过野猪,
凶猛不过老虎,
胆小不过麂子,

Book One

And sticks as weapons.
They braved thunderstorms.

The one-eyed human beings
Used leaves for coats
And grass for quilts.
They quenched the thirst with cold water,
And satisfied the stomach with wild fruits,
Bark and roots.
They could not tell sour from sweet,
Or bitter from hot.

The one-eyed human beings
Slept under trees when they felt sleepy,
Groaned under trees when they were sick.
They danced with branches in glee.
Sometimes yelling, Sometimes laughing,
They lived in tears and laughter.

The one-eyed human beings
Came to know the nature of animals:
Humans were not as strong as boars,
Nor as violent as tigers.
They were not as timid as muntjacs,

查姆 // Chamu

善良不过马鹿,
能爬树的是猴子,
没肝胆的是蚂蚁……

青松和果松一起生,
野鸡和鸟雀一起生,
青蛙和石蚌一起生,
家畜和野兽一起生,
人和猴子一起生,
人和野兽混在一起。

独眼睛这代人啊,
猴子和人分不清。
猴子生儿子,
也是独眼睛。
猴子摘野果,
丢给猴儿吃;
猴儿拾野果,
仔细看形状,
猴儿嚼野果,
尝出果子的滋味。

独眼小猴儿,
主意又多心又灵。

Book One

Nor as docile as deer.

Monkeys were good at climbing trees,

And ants did not have livers and gallbladders…

Pines and Korean pines were close to each other.

Pheasants and birds were close to each other.

Frogs and bullfrogs were close to each other.

Domestic animals and wild ones were close to each other.

Humans and monkeys were close to each other.

Humans and animals mixed with each other.

The one-eyed human beings

Looked like monkeys.

Children of monkeys

Also had one eye only.

Monkeys picked fruit,

To feed their kids.

When the kids picked fruit,

They observed the shapes.

When the kids ate fruit,

They savored the tastes.

The one-eyed monkeys

Were quick-minded and nimble.

拔来了秧草,
在果树上结疙瘩;
果树的名字,
用疙瘩来区分;
疙瘩结在树上,
果树慢慢分得清。

独眼睛这代人啊,
没有找到火种,
冷热不知道,
生熟两不分。
他们熬过严寒和酷暑,
他们度过数不清的冬春;
冷水拌野果,
食物尽生吞。

不知过了多少代,
独眼睛这代人,
用石头敲硬果,
溅起火星星。
火星落在树叶上,
野火烧起山林。
果子滚进火堆里,
熟果味更醇。

They collected grass

To make knots,

So that fruit trees could be

Recognized by the different knots.

With knots on the trees,

People could identify different trees.

The one-eyed human beings

Did not know how to make a fire.

They had no idea about heat and cold,

Nor could they tell raw food from cooked food.

They survived intense heat and severe cold,

And survived innumerable years.

They drank cold water,

Ate wild fruit and raw food.

After many many generations,

The one-eyed human beings

Used stones to crack nuts.

This produced sparks,

Which fell on leaves,

And set fire to groves.

Fruits dropped into the fire

And tasted better than raw ones.

聪明的独眼人,
把火的好处记在心。
用火来御寒冷,
用火来作伴侣,
用火来烧东西……
生吃树果有生味,
熟吃树果味更美。
从此冷暖能分辨,
从此生熟能分清。

独眼睛这代人,
茹苦含辛,
不知道种粮食,
人类难生存。

神仙之王涅侬倮佐颇,
仙王入黄炸当地,
龙王罗阿玛,
水王罗塔纪,
一齐来商量,
共同出主意:
"龙要放出来,
雨要落下地;

上部
Book One

The smart one-eyed human beings

Came to know fire's benefits.

They kept warm by the fire,

They saw fire as their companion,

They cooked with fire …

Raw fruit had a fresh flavor,

Cooked fruit tasted better.

From then on, they could tell heat from cold,

As well as raw food from cooked food.

The one-eyed human beings

Had a hard life.

Not knowing how to grow grain,

It was hard for them to survive.

Nienongluozuopo, the King of the Immortals,

Ruhuangzhadangdi, the Fairy King,

Luo'ama, the Dragon Queen,

And Luotaji, the Water Goddess,

Gathered together to discuss the problem,

And came up with these ideas:

"Dragons should be released,

So that there would be rain nourishing the land.

粮食种子要撒下，
人才有吃的东西。"

水王罗塔纪，
打开四海门，
放出四海水。
龙王罗阿玛，
四方行风雨。
东方放绿龙，
南方放红龙，
西方放白龙，
北方放黑龙。
四方刮风，
四方播雨。

仙王入黄炸当地，
四方去撒种。
粮食种子丢一把，
粮种遍地长，
人间处处有食粮。
树木种子撒一筐，
树木遍山岗，
彝家山寨树木密，
是因种树撒得多。

Rice must be sowed,

So that there would be food for humans."

Luotaji, the Water Goddess,

Opened the gates of all the seas,

And released water on all sides.

Luo'ama, the Dragon Queen, blew wind

And poured rain in the four directions.

She released the green dragon in the east,

The red dragon in the south,

The white dragon in the west,

And the black dragon in the north.

Wind blew in the four directions,

Rain poured down on four sides.

Ruhuangzhadangdi, the Fairy King,

Went to sow in the four directions.

He scattered a handful of seeds,

And crops grew everywhere,

Thus there was food for all.

A basket of tree seeds he threw,

All over the mountains trees grew.

The Yi villages were full of trees,

Because so many tree seeds had been sown.

查姆 // Chamu

龙王罗阿玛，
舀起四瓢水：
东方浇瓢绿龙水，
刮风又下雨，
种子冒嫩芽，
草木叶新蕊。
雨下到的地方，
庄稼都抽穗。

南方浇瓢红龙水，
刮风又下雨，
百花竞开松柏翠；
有雨的地方，
桑麻甘蔗节节生。

西方浇瓢白龙水，
刮风又下雨，
雾露全散尽，
种子落土里。
风吹到的地方，
蜂飞蝶舞百鸟啼；
雨落到的地方，
土地湿润冒清水。

Luo'ama, the Dragon Queen,

Scooped four ladles of water:

She poured a ladle of green dragon water in the east,

There was wind and rain,

Tender leaves grew out of the seeds,

And new pistils appeared on grass and trees.

Where it was raining,

Crops were sprouting.

In the south she ladled red dragon water,

It became windy and rainy,

Flowers were in bloom and trees flourished.

Where it was rainy,

Mulberry, hemp and sugarcane were growing.

In the west she poured a ladle of white dragon water,

Wind started to blew and it rained,

The mist disappeared,

Seeds were sown.

Where wind was blowing,

Bees flew, butterflies danced and birds chirped.

Where it was raining,

The soil became wet and clear water bubbled.

查姆 // Chamu

北方浇瓢黑龙水，
刮风又下雨，
草木常开花，
枯树发新枝；
风吹到的地方，
桃李含苞开鲜花；
雨下到的地方，
枝头果实累累。

四方浇了四瓢水，
四季有风又有雨，
山山流出清泉水，
五谷种得成。

独眼睛时代，
世上万物样样有：
一颗米有鸡蛋大，
谷子长得像竹林；
一粒苞谷鸭蛋大，
苞谷秆子高过房顶；
一颗蚕豆鹅蛋大，
蚕豆苗棵高过人。

In the north she poured a ladle of black dragon water,

It became windy and rainy,

Plants flowered,

New branches grew on old trees.

Where wind was blowing,

Peaches and plums were ready to blossom;

Where it was raining,

The branches were heavy with fruit.

The four ladles of water were poured in the four directions,

There was wind and rain during the four seasons,

Out of every mountain springs flew,

And out of the land the grain grew.

In the one-eyed generation,

There was enough of everything:

Rice grain were as big as chicken eggs,

Their stalks as tall as bamboo trees.

Corn kernels were as big as duck eggs,

Their branches as tall as houses;

Broad beans were as big as goose eggs,

Their stalks as tall as humans.

查姆 // Chamu

独眼睛这代人,
不分男和女,
不分长幼尊卑;
不分白天黑夜,
不分月大月小,
不分秋夏冬春。
怪事天天有,
灾难月月生。
马乱踢人,
牛乱顶人,
鸡乱啄人,
到处乱纷纷。

仙王入黄炸当地,
手摇娑罗枝,
风雨当马骑。
来到泽梗子①,
来到黑夺方②。
找来独眼人,
吩咐他管理这代人:
"你管三千九百年,
一年四季要分明。

---
① 泽梗子:地名。
② 黑夺方:地名。

Book One

In the one-eyed generation,

No distinctions were made between men and women.

Nor between the old and the young,

Nor between day and night,

Nor between longer and shorter months,

Nor between the seasons.

Every day weird things happened,

Every month disasters occurred.

Horses kicked people,

Oxen attacked people,

Roosters pecked people,

The world was full of trouble.

Ruhuangzhadangdi, the Fairy King,

Held a sala branch in hand.

Riding on the wind,

He arrived at Zegengzi[①]

And Heiduofang[②].

He found a one-eyed person,

And asked him to manage the world:

"You will be in charge for 3900 years,

The four seasons must be distinguished.

---

① Zegengzi: the name of a place.
② Heiduofang: the name of a place.

年头月尾要分清,
撒种收割要分清,
世上的人归你管,
你把道理说给众人听。"

独眼睛这代人,
辜负了仙王一片心。
他不过问昼夜,
年月他不分;
太阳月亮他不看,
四季分不清;
播种收割他不管,
庄稼杂草遍地生。

独眼睛这代人,
道理也不讲,
长幼也不分;
儿子不养爹妈,
爹妈不管儿孙。
饿了就互相撕吃,
吵嘴又打架,
时时起纠纷。

神仙之王涅侬倮佐颇,

Book One

Years and months must be separated,
Sowing and harvesting must be made clear.
You must govern all the people,
And teach them to be reasonable."

The one-eyed generation
Let the Fairy Queen down.
They never paid attention to day and night,
Nor distinguished between years and months,
Nor observed the sun and the moon,
Nor divided the four seasons.
They didn't care about sowing or harvesting,
Grain and weeds grew together.

The one-eyed generation
Were not reasonable people.
They did not respect the old.
Children did not look after their aged parents,
Nor did parents take care of their descendants.
When they were hungry, people ate each other.
They quarreled and fought with each other,
And always had disputes.

Nienongluozuopo, the King of the Immortals,

仙王入黄炸当地，
龙王罗阿玛，
水王罗塔纪，
一齐来商量，
共同出主意：
"独眼睛这代人心不好，
要换掉这代人。
要找好心人，
重新繁衍子孙。"

入黄炸当地，
驾着风雨乘着云，
来到泽梗子，
来到黑夺方，
他扮作"讨饭人"，
沿村去乞讨，
查访好心人。

"讨饭人"见人就下跪，
磕头又作揖：
"好心的人啊，
我肚子又饿口又渴，
给点东西填肚子，
给点东西润嘴唇！"

Ruhuangzhadangdi, the Fairy King,

Luo'ama, the Dragon Queen,

Luotaji, the Water Goddess,

Gathered together to discuss the problem.

They came up with these ideas:

The one-eyed generation were not good.

They must be replaced

By kind-hearted people,

Who would produce a new generation."

Ruhuangzhadangdi,

Riding on wind, rain and cloud,

Arrived at Zegengzi

And Heiduofang.

He was disguised as a "beggar",

In the villages he begged,

He tried to find good people.

The "beggar" knelt down whenever he saw people.

He bowed and begged:

"Kind-hearted,

I am hungry and thirsty.

Please give me something to eat,

Please give me something to drink!"

独眼睛人呀,
不给他饭,
不给他水,
张嘴就骂他,
伸手就打他,
出脚就踢他,
把"讨饭人"撵出门。

"讨饭人"又走了一家,
磕头又作揖:
"好心的兄弟呀,
我肚子又饿口又渴,
给点东西填肚子,
给点冷水润润唇!"

那一家人呀,
不给他饭,
不给他水,
不给东西还乱骂,
拳打脚踢推出门。

"讨饭人"走到大路旁,
遇上一个做活人。

A one-eyed person
Did not give him food,
Nor water,
But cursed him,
Beat him,
And kicked him
Out of the house.

The "beggar" knocked on another house.
He bowed and begged:
"Kind-hearted brother,
I am hungry and thirsty.
Please give me something to eat.
Please give me some water to drink!"

That family
Did not give him food,
Nor water,
But cursed him,
And kicked him out.

The "beggar" went to the main road,
And ran into a peasant on the way.

他做活没有牛,
木棒来耕耘,
累得满面汗淋淋。
"讨饭人"走上前,
叩头又作揖:
"好心的阿哥呀,
我肚饿口又渴,
给点东西填肚子,
给点冷水润润唇!"

做活人扶起"讨饭人":
"出门的阿哥啊,
天上鹰顾鹰,
地上苦人帮苦人。
饿了同我吃野果,
渴了和我喝凉水。
野果当饭味道甜,
凉水解渴爽透心。"

"讨饭人"忙道谢:
"我不吃你的野果,
我不喝你的凉水,
世上所有的人,
数你最讲理;

Book One

He ploughed without the help of a bull:
A wooden stick was what he used.
He was panting and sweating.
The "beggar" went up to him,
Bowed and begged:
"Kind-hearted brother,
I am hungry and thirsty.
Please give me something to eat,
Please give me some water to drink!"

The peasant helped the "beggar" to his feet:
"Dear brother, you are away from home.
Hawks in the sky take care of each other,
So poor people on the earth help each other.
We have wild fruit to eat,
We have cold water to drink.
Wild fruit tastes sweet,
Cold water feels cool."

The "beggar" thanked him:
"I will not eat your fruit,
I will not drink your water,
Among all the people in the world,
You are the most good-natured.

世上所有的人,
数你最有良心。

"我把实话告诉你:
在这块天下,
在这块地上,
独眼睛这代人要不得,
要换掉这代人;
干旱要降临,
万物晒死活不成。"

做活人忙询问:
"世上遭干旱,
世上人要绝,
到底咋个整?
请您来指引!"

"讨饭人"笑盈盈:
"阿哥莫忧虑,
阿哥莫担心,
我把葫芦送给你。
葫芦里有喝不完的水,
葫芦里有吃不尽的粮,
还有长生不老药。

Among all the people in the world,
You are the most kind-hearted.

"I will tell you the truth:
In this world,
On this land,
The one-eyed generation is not good-natured,
And must be replaced.
A drought is coming,
Bringing death to everything."

The peasant hastened to ask:
"The world is to dry out,
Human beings are to die out,
What could be done?
Please tell us what should be done!"

The "beggar" smiled:
"My dear brother, don't you worry,
Don't you feel uneasy.
I will give you a gourd.
The water in it will never run out.
Neither will the food,
And an elixir as well.

你一天喝一口水，
你一天吃一把米。
灾难来了你进葫芦去，
三年不会缺水，
三年不会饿肚子。"

"讨饭人"解下葫芦，
做活人接过宝贝，
只听一阵风声起，
不见了"讨饭人"的踪影。

Every day, you can drink some water,

Every day, you can eat some rice.

You can hide yourself in it when disaster comes.

For three years, you will not be short of water,

For three years, you will not be in want of food."

The "beggar" untied the gourd,

The peasant accepted it.

After a gust of wind,

The "beggar" disappeared.

第三章　直眼睛时代

一、干旱来临

天上水门关了,
四方水门关了。
三年见不到闪电,
三年听不到雷声,
三年不刮一阵清风,
三年不洒一滴甘霖。

大地晒干了,
草木渐渐凋零;
大地晒裂了,
地上烟尘滚滚;
大海晒涸了,
鱼虾化成泥;
江河晒干了,
沙石碎成灰;
老虎豹子晒死,

上部
Book One

Canto 3   The Vertical-Eyed Era

I. The Coming of the Drought

The water gate in the sky was closed,

The water gates in the four directions were shut.

For three years, there was no lightning,

There was no thunder,

There was not even a breeze,

There was not even a raindrop.

The earth dried up,

Grass and trees gradually withered.

The earth cracked,

The air was dusty.

The sea dried up,

Fish and shrimp turned into mud.

Rivers and lakes dried up,

Sand and stones turned into ashes.

Tigers and leopards were scorched,

马鹿岩羊晒绝，
不见雀鸟展翅，
不见蛇蝎爬行；
飞禽走兽绝迹，
大地荒凉天昏沉。

顶天柱被晒断，
三座大山被晒塌，
星星晒得出汗，
月亮晒出泪水，
娑罗树晒得枯黄。

众神之王涅侬倮佐颇，
仙王入黄炸当地，
龙王罗阿玛，
水王罗塔纪，
还有罗塔纪的姑娘，
一齐来商量，
共同出主意：
"天旱三年，
江河干涸，
大地开裂，
草木枯萎，
玉石俱焚，

Book One

Deer and blue sheep were seared,

There were no birds or sparrows flying,

There were no snakes and scorpions crawling.

Birds and animals became extinct,

The sky was gloomy and the earth desolate.

The sky-supporting pole toppled,

The three mountains collapsed,

The stars sweated,

The moon shed tears,

And the sala tree was scorched.

Nienongluozuopo, the King of the Immortals,

Ruhuangzhadangdi, the Fairy King,

Luo'ama, the Dragon Queen,

Luotaji, the Water Goddess,

And Princess of Luotaji,

Had a discussion

To find a solution:

"The drought has lasted three years,

Rivers and lakes have dried up,

The earth cracked,

Grass and trees withered,

Jade and stone were both burnt to ashes,

查姆 // Chamu

独眼人晒死。
要留'做活人',
做大地的主人。"

入黄炸当地,
驾着风雨乘着云,
寻找好心人;
东边西边找,
南边北边寻,
不见那个做活人。

仙王来到泽梗子,
仙王来到黑夺方,
四方巡查遍,
不见一个人影。
仿佛有雀鸟在飞,
好像有什么在唱?
仙王仔细瞧,
只见蜜蜂扇翅膀;
仙王仔细听,
听到蜜蜂嗡嗡唱。

仙王开口问:
小蜜蜂啊小蜜蜂,

The one-eyed people died from the heat.
The 'peasant' must be saved
To be the master of the world."

Ruhuangzhadangdi,
Riding on wind, rain and clouds,
Tried to find the kind-hearted peasant.
He searched here and there,
He searched everywhere,
Without seeing the peasant.

The Fairy King came to Zegengzi;
The Fairy King came to Heiduofang.
He searched here and there,
Without seeing anyone anywhere.
There seemed to be birds flying,
There seemed to be someone singing?
The Fairy King looked closely,
And saw bees fluttering.
He listened carefully,
And heard bees humming.

He asked immediately:
"Little bees, Little bees,

你飞西又飞东,
你略遇见做活人?"

蜜蜂嗡嗡把话讲:
"苏罗赛文地方,
赛措山头上,
有两棵香樟树,
树上有一对猴子,
树上有斑鸠一双,
树下有两个石头,
石头旁边有两蓬青草,
青草旁边有一对牛羊,
牛羊旁边有猪狗一对。
大树下,石头上,
不见做活人,
倒是坐着一个独眼郎。
他一无弟妹,
二无父母,
三无兄长,
独自一人甚凄凉。

"这个独眼人嘛,
烈日没有把他晒伤;
他时而烦闷,

You have been flying here and there.

Have you seen the peasant anywhere?"

The bees hummed:

"There is a place called Suluosaiwen,

Where Saicuo Mountain lies.

On its top there are two camphor trees,

On which there are a pair of monkeys,

And a pair of turtledoves.

Under the trees there are two stones.

Near the stones there are two patches of grass.

Near the grass there are a couple of oxen and sheep.

Nearby there are a couple of pigs and dogs.

Under the tree and on the stones,

The peasant cannot be seen,

But there is an one-eyed man sitting there.

He has no younger brothers or sisters,

Nor parents,

Nor elder brothers.

He is lonely and alone.

"The one-eyed man

Did not suffer from the scorching sun.

Sometimes he was bored,

他时而歌唱。
他撒尿在树下，
枯树披绿装；
尿滴在石头上，
石头长出青苔；
尿水落在青草上，
青草嫩汪汪；
牛羊吃了青草，
牛羊更肥壮；
猪狗吃了青草，
猪狗免病伤；
猴子吃了树果，
猴子林中最欢畅；
斑鸠吃了果子，
斑鸠能展翅飞翔；
蜜蜂采了树花，
蜜蜂先把蜜糖尝。"

仙王听了蜜蜂的话，
很快来到苏罗赛文地方，
很快来到赛措山头上。
他在两棵树下，
果然寻到独眼郎。

Sometimes he was singing.

When he peed under the trees,

The withered trees revived.

When his urine dripped on the stones,

Moss grew on them.

When his urine dripped on the grass,

It grew tender and green.

The oxen and sheep ate the grass,

And became fat and sturdy.

The pigs and dogs ate the grass,

And became healthy.

The monkeys ate the fruit from the tree,

And became agile.

The turtledoves ate the fruit from the tree,

And could fly high.

The bees gathered tree flowers,

And were the first to taste honey."

Hearing that, the Fairy King

Rushed to Suluosaiwen,

And reached the top of Saicuo Mountain.

Under the two trees,

He found the one-eyed man.

独眼人见了仙王,

磕头又作揖,

热泪滚滚话儿长:

"神仙呵,救命的恩人!

万里路上不见人,

伴我的只有太阳;

千里路上不见树,

只剩两棵香樟;

百里路上无飞鸟,

只有斑鸠低声唱;

树上不见虫鸣,

只有蜜蜂采花忙;

十里路上不见走兽,

只有猪狗一对,

只有牛羊一双;

五里路上找不到粮和水,

只有葫芦里的一点水和粮。

我对着大地呼救,

回答我的只有风声簌簌响。

究竟谁能把晒焦的大地变样?

究竟谁能和我做伴成双?

"独水难流淌,

独鸟难飞翔,

At the sight of the Fairy King,

The one-eyed man knelt and bowed.

In tears he said:

"Oh, Fairy King, my savior!

There is nobody within ten thousand miles.

The sun is my only companion.

There are no trees within one thousand miles,

Except two camphor trees.

There are no birds within one hundred miles,

Except the singing turtledoves.

No insects could be seen on the trees,

Except the honey-gathering bees.

There are no animals within ten miles,

Except a couple of pigs and dogs,

And a couple of oxen and sheep.

No rice or water can be found for five miles,

Except a little in the gourd.

I shouted for help,

But the only response was the rustling of the wind.

Who on earth can relieve the world from the drought?

Who on earth will be my better half?

It's difficult for a single stream to flow on.

It's difficult for a single bird to fly far.

独木不成林,
独花难飘香,
独个巴掌拍不响,
独人难抗旱魔和灾荒。
恩人呵,神仙!
你能腾云驾雾,
求求你设法解旱荒!"

仙王开口把话讲:
"好心人啊不用慌,
十天之内有人来,
知心朋友会帮忙,
有人伴你会成双。"
说罢驾着清风腾空去,
飞回缥缈太空中。

仙王派出姑娘撒赛歇,
来到苏罗赛文地方,
来到赛措山上,
来到独眼人身旁。

独眼人一见仙姑娘,
愁容变笑脸,
忙把客人迎进房:

It's impossible for one tree to make a forest.

It's difficult for one flower to give out fragrance.

It's impossible for one hand to clap.

It's difficult for one man to fight drought and disaster.

Oh, my savior, my god!

You can ride on clouds and wind,

Please try to defeat the drought!"

The Fairy King said:

"Kind-hearted man, don't panic,

Within ten days someone will be here.

This bosom friend will help you,

And be your companion."

Then he rode on the clear wind and vanished.

Back into the misty universe he flew.

The Fairy King sent his daughter Fairy Sasaixie,

To the place named Suluosaiwen.

She arrived at Saicuo Mountain,

And found the one-eyed man.

Seeing the Fairy Princess,

The man's sad look turned into smile,

He welcomed the guest into his shelter:

"亲亲的阿姐呀,
我这里没有板凳,
请坐树叶上;
我这里没有水喝,
只有葫芦水;
我这里没有粮食,
请把野果尝一尝。"

仙姑娘说:
"不喝你的葫芦水,
不吃你的救命粮。"
她把独眼人细打量:
独眼人头发白得像棉花,
头上还有瓦雀窝;
全身黑得像栎炭,
身上有虮子,
脸像干树叶一样黄;
眉毛长得像茅草蓬,
眉毛丛中有野蜂;
手指像竹节,
手皮粗得像松树皮;
脚像龙爪子,
脚裂有筷子宽,
脚裂里有麻蛇,

"My dear sister,

I have no stool.

Please sit on the leaves.

I have no water to drink,

Except a little from the gourd.

I have no rice to eat.

Please have some wild fruit instead."

The Fairy Princess said:

"I'm not drinking your water,

I'm not eating your precious rice."

She looked the one-eyed man up and down:

His hair was as white as cotton.

There was a sparrow's nest on his head.

He was as black as coal.

His skin was covered with lice.

His face was as haggard as dried leaves.

His eyebrows were as messy as grass,

And on them there were wild bees.

His fingers were as tough as bamboo joints.

His hand skin was as rough as pine bark.

His feet were as rough as dragon claws.

The cracks on his feet were as wide as chopsticks,

So wide that snakes were crawling in them.

脚板上有石蚌；
穿的是棕树皮，
远看像囤箩。
仙姑娘越看越难看，
乘着雾露飞上了天。

涅侬倮佐颇，
召集众神仙来商量：
"还是请罗塔纪姑娘，
下到地上去帮忙。"

罗塔纪姑娘，
舀了四瓢水，
来到苏罗赛文地方，
来到赛措山上。
她拿根棍子，
指着独眼人头上的瓦雀，
"你去树上做窝。"
指着眉毛上的野蜂，
"你去悬崖上落脚。"
指着肚子上的虮子，
"你去老箐里生活。"
指着脚缝里的麻蛇，
"你到空心树里去住。"

Frogs could be seen on his feet.

Wearing palm bark,

He looked like a basket from a distance.

The more she looked, the uglier he appeared.

She rode on the clouds and fled.

Nienongluozuopo

Called all gods together to discuss it:

"It's better to ask Princess Luotaji

To go down and help."

Princess Luotaji

Scooped four ladles of water,

Came to Suluosaiwen,

And arrived at Saicuo Mountain.

With a stick in her hand, she pointed at the sparrow

On the one-eyed man's head,

"Go and nest in trees."

She pointed at the wild bees on his eyebrows,

"Go and live on the cliffs."

She pointed at the lice on his belly,

"Go and live in the valley."

She pointed at the snake in the cracks of his feet,

"Go and live in hollow trees."

指着脚板上的石蚌，
　"你到沟塘里唱歌。"

罗塔纪姑娘，
对独眼人讲：
　"好心的做活人啊，
你不用焦虑，
我给你带来四瓢水，
你快拿去洗身子。"

独眼人接过四瓢水，
一瓢水洗头发，
白发变黑发；
一瓢水洗手，
粗手变嫩手；
一瓢水洗脚，
脚裂合拢了，
行路似风响；
一瓢水洗身子，
污垢全洗净，
独眼睛变成直眼睛，
鼻子剪刀样，
下巴鸡蛋圆，
嘴唇像鹦哥，

上部
Book One

She pointed at the frog on his feet,
"Go and sing in the pond."

Princess Luotaji
Said to the one-eyed man:
"Kind peasant,
Don't you worry.
I have brought four ladles of water
For you to wash yourself."

The one-eyed man took the water.
He washed his hair with one ladle of it,
And his white hair turned black.
He washed his hands with another ladle,
And his rough hands became tender.
He washed his feet with a third ladle,
The cracks on his feet were healed,
And he could walk like the wind.
He washed his body with the fourth ladle,
The dirt was cleaned off,
His one eye turned into two vertical eyes,
His nose was like a pair of scissors,
His jaw was as round as an egg,
His lips were like those of a parrot,

脸上闪红光,
老人变成少年郎。

罗塔纪姑娘,
给直眼人打扮梳妆。
给他取下树叶帽,
给他取下树叶裳;
叫他脱去绿叶裤,
全身换新装。
蝴蝶围着他飞,
蜜蜂围着他唱。

直眼睛人呀,
望着罗塔纪姑娘,
两脚跪下地,
两手忙作揖:
"仙姑娘啊仙姑娘,
我用什么感激你?"

罗塔纪姑娘,
只笑不回答,
彩云当马骑,
回到了天上。
她把直眼人的美貌,

Book One

His face was glowing red:
The old man became a young lad.

Princess Luotaji
Helped dress the vertical-eyed man.
She took off his leaf-hat,
She took off his leaf-clothes,
She asked him to take off his leaf-pants,
She dressed him in new clothes.
Butterflies were flying around him,
Bees were singing about him.

The vertical-eyed man,
Looked at Princess Luotaji,
Fell on his knees,
Bowed and said:
"Oh, My Goddess, My Goddess,
How can I express my gratitude?"

Princess Luotaji
Smiled without saying anything.
She rode on the colorful clouds,
To heaven she returned.
She told Fairy Sasaixie,

告诉仙姑娘撒赛歇。

仙姑撒赛歇,
重返苏罗赛文地方,
重回赛措山上。
她找到了直眼人,
看他打扮不一样:
肩套黑领褂,
身穿白布衣,
鞋子三道花,
头戴竹蔑帽,
一身新衣裳。
他用棍子打树果,
敲下树果做食粮。

仙姑娘撒赛歇,
高高兴兴开了腔:
"摘果的人呀,
请问是男还是女?
是男嘿咯有妻子?
是女嘿咯有丈夫?"

直眼人忙回答:
"世上只剩我一人,

Book One

About the vertical-eyed man's charisma.

Fairy Sasaixie

Returned to Suluosaiwen,

To Saicuo Mountain.

She found the vertical-eyed man,

Who was in new garments:

He wore a black vest

On top of a white cotton coat.

His shoes were embroidered with flower patterns,

He wore a sawali hat.

He was dressed in new clothes.

He used a stick to get fruit from the trees,

Which filled his trays.

Fairy Sasaixie

Spoke happily:

"The person picking the tree's fruit,

Are you a man or a woman?

If you are a man, do you have a wife?

If you are a woman, do you have a husband?"

The vertical-eyed man answered right away:

"In this world I am the only man,

我是没有妻子的孤苦人!"

"阿哥啊阿哥,
世上只有我一个女人,
我有话儿问问你,
要是答对了,
我俩做夫妻。"

直眼人忙点头,
"先请阿妹唱。"

"阿哥啊,阿哥!
世上不放盐能吃的是哪样?
地上不撒种能结果的是哪样?
山上不用栽种能捡来吃的是哪样?
不用喂养能吃肉的是哪样?
有嘴不说话的是哪样?
无嘴响四方的是哪样?
知道白天黑夜的是哪样?
……"

"阿姐呀,阿姐!
世上不放盐能吃的是果子,
地上不撒种能结果的是野地瓜,

Book One

I am a lonely, wifeless man!"

"My dear brother,
I am the only woman in this world.
I want to ask you some questions.
If you can answer them right,
We can get married."

The vertical-eyed man nodded his head,
"Dear sister, please go ahead."

"Dear brother,
What can be eaten without salt?
What can bear fruit without sowing?
What can be harvested without planting?
What can provide meat without being fed?
What is it that can't speak with a mouth?
What is it that can make sounds without a mouth?
What knows about day and night…"

"My dear sister,
Fruit can be eaten without salt,
Wild melons can bear fruit without sowing,

山中不栽种能捡来吃的是菌子,
不喂养能拿肉来吃的是野兽鱼虾。
有嘴不说话的是坛子,
无嘴响四方的是唢呐,
知道白天黑夜的是公鸡。
阿姐呀,我说的对不对?
要是说对啦,
我俩做一家!"

仙姑娘眯眯笑,
点头不说话。
他们来到两棵香樟树下,
对着大树磕头作揖。
认一棵树做爹,
认一棵树做娘;
请两棵树作证,
他俩成亲做夫妻。

仙姑娘告诉直眼人,
就选树下作房基,
两人动手盖新房。
妻子去割茅草,
丈夫去砍屋梁。
青石作墙脚,

Mushrooms can be harvested without planting,
Wild animals and fish provide meat without being fed.
The jar can't speak with a mouth,
Suona makes sounds without a mouth,
The rooster knows about day and night.
Dear sister, am I right?
If I am right,
Let us get married!"

Fairy Sasaixie smiled,
And nodded without a word.
They went to the two camphor trees,
Bowed and knelt down before them.
One tree was regarded as their father,
The other as their mother.
The trees were the witnesses
Of their marriage.

Fairy Sasaixie told the vertical-eyed man,
They should build a house under the trees.
The couple started the task.
The wife went to collect thatch,
The husband went to get pillars.
Stones were used for the base,

查姆 // Chamu

树枝作椽子，
树叶当瓦片，
树皮当板墙。
两人忙碌了九天，
两人辛苦了九夜，
盖成一间新房。
山雀有窝喳喳叫，
人有住房喜洋洋。

猴子把树果抢吃完了，
他们没有充饥的食粮。
鸟兽把泉水喝干了，
箐里没有泉水流淌。
白狗在门外汪汪哭，
从白天哭到夜晚，
从夜晚哭到天亮，
哭声震动了诸神王。

涅依倮佐颇召集众神仙，
一齐出主意：
再叫罗塔纪姑娘，
舀来四瓢水，
放进五谷种，
四瓢水泼向大地，

Branches were used for rafters,

Leaves were used for tiles,

Bark was used for the walls.

For nine days the couple sweated,

For nine nights the couple worked,

And the new house was completed.

When sparrows have a nest, they chirp,

When people have a house, they rejoice.

Monkeys ate all the tree fruit,

The couple had nothing to eat.

Birds and animals drank all spring water,

There was no water flowing in the valley.

Outside, the white dog was barking and crying,

From morning to evening,

From evening to morning.

Its cry moved all the gods.

Nienongluozuopo summoned all the gods

To find a solution:

Princess Luotaji was asked

To ladle four scoops of water,

And put grain seeds in it.

The water was splashed over the earth,

五谷种撒向四方,
地上有了种子,
地上有了雨水。

种子落在大门口,
白狗把种子衔进屋里,
见了仙姑夫妇俩,
摇头摆尾喜得狂。

两夫妇低头看:
"啊,有了种子,
就有食粮;
有了种子啊,
生存就有了希望。"

两人把种子晒了三天,
两人把种子泡了三夜。
种子撒下地,
一颗发三苗,
一苗生两叶,
幼苗嫩汪汪。

过了一个月,
禾苗绿茵茵,

Book One

Grains seeds were scattered with the water.
Now there were seeds
And rain water on the ground.

Seeds fell in front of the house.
The white dog took them in.
When it saw the couple,
It wagged its tail with joy.

The couple looked down and saw the seeds:
"Ah, with seeds,
We will have crops.
With seeds,
We will have hope."

The couple dried the seeds in the sun for three days,
The couple soaked the seeds in water for three nights.
Then they sowed the seeds.
Three seedlings grew out of each seed.
Two leaves grew on each seedling.
The seedlings were full of life.

After a month,
The seedlings became lush.

过了三个月，
谷穗黄生生。
谷子比人高，
一棵谷子生九穗，
一穗谷子有苞谷长。
一丛谷子收九箩，
九箩谷子堆满仓。
苞谷长有房子高，
一棵苞谷背三包，
一包苞谷有手长，
一粒苞谷鸡蛋大，
一棵能收三箩筐。
高粱有大树高，
一棵高粱结三穗，
一穗高粱马尾长，
一颗高粱有核桃大，
一棵高粱收九缸。
夫妇忙收粮，
装满九间房；
夫妇尝新谷，
越吃饭越香。

Book One

After three months,

Millet ears became yellow.

The millet was taller than humans.

On each millet stalk grew nine ears.

The millet ears were as big as corn ears.

A patch of millet harvested nine baskets of seeds,

Which filled up one barn.

Corn was as tall as the houses,

On each stalk grew three corn ears,

Which were as long as arms,

And the corn was as big as eggs.

One stalk harvested three baskets of corn.

Sorghum was as big as trees,

On each stalk grew three ears,

Which were as long as horse tails,

The sorghum seeds were as big as walnuts,

A sorghum stalk harvested nine vats.

The couple was busy with harvesting crops,

Which filled up nine rooms;

The couple tasted the new grain,

The more they ate, the tastier they felt it was.

二、直眼睛人

撒赛歇和直眼人,
结成夫妻做一家,
日子过得美满,
只愁不生娃娃。

忽然一天夜晚,
仙姑娘肚子疼了,
她生下个皮口袋,
袋里传出哝哝呀呀的声音,
好像娃娃在说话,
不知是男还是女?

撒赛歇听了难过:
"生了个大口袋,
实在羞人啰!"
她看着皮口袋,
从白天哭到夜晚,
从夜晚哭到白天。
哭声传到天上,
被龙王罗阿玛听见,
他派下撒赛萨若埃姑娘:

II. The Vertical-Eyed Man

Fairy Sasaixie and the vertical-eyed man
Got married and formed a family.
They enjoyed happiness,
But they were childless.

Then one evening,
The Fairy had a bellyache,
And gave birth to a leather bag,
Out of which came a babbling voice,
Like a baby speaking.
Was it a boy or a girl?

Fairy Sasaixie felt very sad:
"I gave birth to a big bag.
How shameful!"
She looked at the leather bag,
Crying from morning to evening,
And from evening to morning.
Her cries traveled to heaven,
And were heard by Luo'ama, the Dragon Queen,
She sent down Sasaisaruoai, who said:

查姆 // Chamu

"莫伤心啊,莫流泪,
我来看看究竟生了个啥?"

撒赛萨若埃拿出大剪刀,
把口袋剪成三节,
袋里跳出一群小蚂蚱。
上节四十个,
中节四十个,
下节四十个,
蚂蚱跳三跳,
变成一百二十个胖娃娃。

他们都有两只眼睛,
两只眼睛亮晶晶,
不到一月会说话,
不到二月能走路,
一年就能扛犁耙。
他们是"拉爹"的后代,
他们的名字叫"拉拖"。

一百二十个小"拉拖",
儿子有六十个,
姑娘有六十个。
儿子大了爱玩泥,

Book One

"Don't cry and don't be sad,

I am here to see what is inside?"

Sasaisaruoai took out scissors,

And cut the bag into three parts.

Grasshoppers jumped out:

Forty jumped from the upper part,

Forty jumped from the middle part,

Forty jumped from the lower part,

The grasshoppers jumped three times,

And turned into one hundred and twenty chubby kids.

They all had two eyes,

Like twinkling stars.

Within one month they could talk,

Within two months they could walk,

Within one year they could plow,

They were the descendants of Ladie.

They were named Latuo.

Of the one hundred and twenty young Latuo,

Sixty were boys,

Sixty were girls.

When grown up, the boys loved to play with mud,

查姆 // Chamu

姑娘大了爱采花；
儿子上山开火地，
姑娘河边种桑麻；
儿子长大喜欢姑娘，
姑娘长大催着成家。
世上只有这群兄妹。
兄妹只好成亲做一家。

上节口袋生的四十个，
配成二十家，
去高山种桑麻；
中节口袋生的四十个，
配成二十家，
去坝子种谷、种瓜；
下节口袋生的四十个，
配成二十家，
去河边打鱼捞虾。
兄妹一百二十人，
配成六十家，
一家住一处，
一处一寨隔有篱笆。

过了九千七百年，
世上住不下，

Book One

When grown up, the girls loved to pick flower buds;

The boys went to the mountains to practice slash and burn,

The girls went to the valleys to plant mulberry and hemp;

The boys wanted to have girl-friends when they grew up,

The girls wanted to get married when they grew up.

These brothers and sisters were the only people in the world.

They had to get married and become couples.

Forty brothers and sisters from the upper part

Formed twenty couples

And went to the mountains to plant mulberry and hemp;

Forty brothers and sisters from the middle part

Formed twenty couples

And went to the flat land to plant melons and crops;

Forty brothers and sisters from the lower part

Formed twenty couples,

And went to the riverside to fish.

These one hundred and twenty people

Formed sixty couples.

Each couple lived in a different place,

Each place became a village with fences.

After nine thousand and seven hundred years,

The world became too crowded to live in,

查姆 // Chamu

直眼人一天比一天增多,
地方一天比一天窄狭。

直眼睛这代人呀,
他们不懂道理,
他们经常吵嘴打架。
各吃各的饭,
各烧各的汤。
一不管亲友,
二不管爹妈。
爹死了拴着脖子丢在山里,
妈死了拴着脚杆抛进沟凹。

众神之王涅侬俫佐颇,
找来龙王罗阿玛,
水王罗塔纪,
还有古木折意巴①,
一齐来商量:
"树多不砍嘛,
看不见青天;
草多不割嘛,
看不见道路;
不讲道理的人不换嘛,

---

① 古木折意巴:又称盘古,参与造天地,重换一代人。

Book One

The vertical-eyed people increased day by day,
Their living space decreased with each passing day.

The vertical-eyed generation
Did not get along with each other.
They quarreled and fought with each other.
They made their own meals,
They cooked their own soup.
They neither cared for relatives or friends,
Nor for their parents.
When their fathers died, they dumped them on the mountain,
When their mothers died, they threw them into the valley.

Nienongluozuopo, the King of the Immortals,
Called for Luo'ama, the Dragon Queen,
Luotaji, the Water Goddess,
And Gumuzheyiba[①],
To have a discussion:
"Too many trees without being cut
Would cover up the sky;
Too much grass without being weeded
Would cover up the road;
Bad people without being replaced

---

① Gumuzheyiba: also known as Pangu, a creator who took part in the creation of the world and the new generation.

看不见善良和淳朴。
要重发一代芽,
要重开一次花,
要重结一次果,
要重换一代人。"

神王和仙王,
水王和龙王,
派了涅侬撒萨歇,
查访好心人。
要让好心人传宗接代,
要一代比一代聪明能干,
要一代比一代兴旺发达。

涅侬撒萨歇,
骑着龙马到人间,
走到半路上,
装着跌折龙马腰,
假称跌断龙马腿,
到处找药医龙马。

东方去了去西方,
南方去了去北方,
四方四十大户,

Would cover up honesty and goodness.
New seeds must be sowed,
New flowers must be produced,
New fruit must be born,
New human beings must be created."

The Fairy Queen and the King of the Immortals,
The Water Goddess and the Dragon Queen,
Sent for Nienongsasaxie,
To look for kind-hearted people.
Only kind-hearted people could have children.
Each generation must be more capable than the last one.
Each generation must be more prosperous than its predecessor.

Nienongsasaxie
Rode on a dragon horse and came to the world.
On his way, he pretended that
His dragon horse's back was broken,
His dragon horse's leg was broken.
He asked for medical aid for his horse everywhere.

From east to west,
From south to north,
In the four directions, there were forty rich families,

家家都访遍。
每到一家要作一百二十个揖,
每到一户要磕一百二十个头。
"大爹大妈呀,
我的龙马腰折啦,
我的龙马腿断啦,
要人血才能医好,
请阿爹阿妈帮帮忙,
我多多谢你家。"

四方四大户,
良心又黑又毒辣:
"莫说人血不给你,
人尿也休想给你医龙马。"

涅侬撒萨歇,
离开大户住的寨子,
再次查访好人家。
他走到十字路口,
碰上一个庄稼人。
庄稼人肩上扛着犁,
手中把牛拉。

涅侬撒萨歇,

上部
Book One

He visited all of them.

He bowed one hundred and twenty times to each family,

He kowtowed one hundred and twenty times to each family.

"Dear Uncle and Aunt,

My dragon horse suffered a fracture in the back,

My dragon house suffered a fracture in the leg.

Only human blood can heal it,

Please help me.

I will be very grateful."

The rich families in the four directions

Were cruel and vicious,

"We won't even give you urine,

Never mind human blood."

Nienongsasaxie

Left the villages of the rich families,

And continued to look for kind-hearted families.

When he arrived at a crossroads,

He ran into a peasant.

A plough he was carrying,

An ox he was leading.

Nielongsasaxie

弯腰又作揖：
"阿哥哟，请你等一等，
问你几句要紧话。"

庄稼人名叫阿朴独姆，
他家里还有一个妹妹。
他看看好心的涅侬撒萨歇，
含笑迎客人：
"过路的阿哥哟，
不用弯腰作揖，
你有难处只管说，
也许我能帮你使点力。"

"我的龙马腰折啦，
我的龙马腿断啦，
要人血才能医好，
求阿哥帮我医龙马。"

"你把金刀拿给我，
你把银碗拿给我，
划开指头给你血，
若要人肉我也能割下。"
阿朴独姆用金针刺出手上血，
交给涅侬撒萨歇。

Bowed and said:

"My dear brother, please don't go,

I have something important to ask you."

The peasant was named Apudumu,

He had a younger sister.

He looked at the kind-hearted Nienongsasaxie,

And said with a smile:

"Dear brother,

Please don't bow to me,

Please don't hesitate to tell me your problem,

Maybe I could help solve it."

"My dragon horse's back had a fracture,

My dragon horse's leg had a fracture,

Only human blood could heal it,

My dear brother, please help me."

"Please give your gold knife to me,

Please give your silver bowl to me,

I will cut my finger and give my blood to you,

I could even give my flesh to you."

Apudumu used a gold needle to make his finger bleed,

And gave Nienongsasaxie his blood.

涅侬撒萨歇，
拉着阿朴独姆，
对他说了真话：
"我走遍九山十八凹，
没见一个好心人，
没遇一户好人家。
你的心像月亮一样干净，
你为人像大树一样正直，
你是世上最好的人。

"直眼睛这代人，
心肠实在差，
要重换一代人，
要重开一次花。
世上只留你们兄妹传后代，
你们要牢牢记住我的话。

"一百二十天内要发大水，
要用洪水洗大地，
要用洪水洗万物。
洗干净大地，万物再生，
洗干净大地，再种庄稼，
洗干净大地，再传后代。"

Book One

Nienongsasaxie

Held Apudumu's hands,

And told him the truth:

"I have trudged nine mountains and eighteen valleys,

Without seeing one nice person

Or one nice family.

Your heart is as clean as the moon,

You are as upright as a tree,

You are the best person in this world.

"The vertical-eyed generation

Are too cold-hearted,

They must be replaced,

New flowers must be produced.

You and your sister are the only humans that will remain.

Please remember what I say.

"Within one hundred and twenty days,

A flood will come,

And wash the land and everything in it.

When the land is washed clean, everything will be recreated,

When the land is washed clean, crops will be sowed again,

When the land is washed clean, a new generation will be born."

第四章　横眼睛时代

一、洪水滔天

洪水要来了，
地暗又天昏，
月亮无光彩，
太阳无光辉。

阿朴独姆兄妹俩，
听说洪水要淹天，
白天叹息落泪，
黑夜焦愁担心。

涅侬撒萨歇问阿朴独姆：
"好心的庄稼人啊，
为啥焦愁不安？
为啥落泪叹息？"

阿朴独姆回答：

Canto 4 The Horizontal-Eyed Generation

I. The Flood

The flood was coming,
The earth and the sky were darkening,
The moon stopped glistening,
The sun stopped glowing.

Apudumu and his sister
Heard that the flood would drown the world,
They sighed and shed tears in the daylight,
They were worried and anxious during the dark night.

Nienongsasaxie asked Apudumu:
"Kind-hearted peasant,
What makes you worry?
What makes you sigh and cry?"

Apudumu answered:

"洪水要来啦,
有金的打金船,
有银的打银船,
有铜的打铜船,
有铁的打铁船,
有锡的打锡船。
我们兄妹俩,
没有金银,
没有铜铁,
用什么来打船?
无船怎能躲过洪水,
无船怎能避开灾难?"

涅依撒萨歇说:
"好心的庄稼人,
你不用忧虑,
你不用叹息。
我给你一颗大瓜种,
这颗瓜种不一般,
一半绿来一半红,
拿在日下晒三天,
拿在月下露三晚,
拿去种在家门前。

"The flood is coming,

People who have gold are making gold boats,

People who have silver are making silver boats,

People who have copper are making copper boats,

People who have iron are making iron boats,

People who have tin are making tin boats.

My sister and I

Have no gold or silver,

Nor copper or iron,

How can we make a boat?

How can we survive the flood without a boat?

How can we survive the disaster without a boat?"

Nienongsasaxie said:

"Kind-hearted peasant,

You don't have to worry,

You don't have to sigh.

I'll give you a big melon seed,

It is not a normal seed,

It is half green and half red.

Dry it for three days in the sunlight,

Expose it for three nights in the moonlight,

Then plant it in front of your house.

"栽后三天勤浇水,
栽后七天壅瓜蔓,
栽后十天搭瓜架,
瓜藤架上串枝连。
瓜藤横爬十八拿,
瓜藤直爬接通天。
藤上结个大葫芦,
你们和葫芦有因缘。

"三月种瓜子,
六月葫芦就长成,
九月葫芦皮变黄,
十月葫芦硬又坚。
腊月摘葫芦,
葫芦有房子大,
挖空葫芦就是船,
你们兄妹住中间。"

阿朴独姆,
心事想不完:
"有了躲洪水的地方,
还缺吃的又怎么办?"

涅依撒萨歇,

"Then water it often within the first three days,
Vines will grow in seven days,
Melon shelves must be set up within ten days,
The shelves will be covered with vines.
Vines will crawl very far horizontally,
Vines will creep vertically to reach the sky.
On the vines will grow a big gourd,
You are destined to be together with the gourd.

"Plant the seed in March,
And the gourd will be ripe in June,
The gourd will turn yellow in September,
The gourd will become strong and hard in October.
The gourd can be harvested in December,
It will be as big as a chamber,
When hollowed inside, it will become a boat,
Where you and your sister can hide."

Apudumu
Had other things to worry about:
"Even though we can hide ourselves in it,
What if we don't have things to eat?"

Nienongsasaxie

开言又指点：
"给你一碗粮，
千万莫吃完，
今日吃了明日长，
明日吃了又还原，
永远吃不完。

"再给你一把种子，
你们要勤耕苦种田。
庄稼遍地长，
粮食吃不完。"

阿朴独姆兄妹俩，
把话记心间。
藏着种子带着粮，
钻进葫芦里面。

勤快的小蜜蜂，
衔来黄蜂蜡，
把葫芦的口封严，
使兄妹俩免遭水淹。

涅侬撒萨歇，
看着她们躲进葫芦里，

上部
Book One

Said to them:

"I'll give you a bowl of rice,

Please don't eat it up.

After you eat some today,

It will grow the next day and every day,

And never be eaten up.

"I'll give you a handful of seeds,

You must work hard to plough the fields.

You will have a bumper harvest,

You will have more than enough to eat."

Apudumu and his sister

Bore the words in mind.

They took the rice and the seeds,

And hid themselves in the gourd.

Buzzing bees

Brought yellow wax

To seal the gourd

And protect them from the flood.

Seeing them hiding in the gourd,

Nienongsasaxie

心中扎实喜欢。
他才吩咐老龙下大雨,
要下得洪水淹到天边。

龙眼眨一眨,
满天乌云翻;
龙尾摆一摆,
天空就扯闪;
龙身抖一抖,
狂风暴雨卷万山。

雨点鸡蛋大,
雨柱似竹竿;
下了七天七夜,
大地茫茫被水淹。
地上波浪滚滚,
波涛直冲云天。

树根飘上天,
浮萍天上转,
乱草裹成团,
天连水,
水连天,
葫芦飘到天上边。

Book One

Felt delighted.

He then asked the old dragon to send rain,

Until the flood covered all the plain.

The dragon blinked his eyes,

Dark clouds started billowing;

The dragon swung his tail,

It started lightning;

The dragon shook his body,

The world was overwhelmed by a thunderstorm.

The raindrops were as big as eggs,

The streams of rain poles were like bamboo tubes.

It rained for seven days and seven nights,

The world was drowned in the flood.

On the earth were billowing waves,

Dashing into the cloudy sky.

Tree roots were flying in the sky,

Duckweeds were spinning about in the air,

Grass became tangled masses,

The sky and the water

Met and touched.

The gourd floated high up.

大鱼想吃星星，
黄鳝在天上乱钻；
石蚌望着月亮乱叫，
虾子围着星星撒欢；
水鸭在天空漫游，
水獭在天际打圈圈。

金船沉海底，
银船沉海底，
铜船沉海底，
铁船、锡船也沉海底。

涅侬倮佐颇，
召集众神仙来商量：
派涅侬撒萨歇，
派罗塔纪姑娘，
还有古木折意巴，
共同治洪水。

古木折意巴，
想出办法治洪水：
东方水门开，
南方水门开，

上部
Book One

Big fish wanted to eat stars,

Eels were moving about in the heavens;

Frogs were croaking toward the moon,

Around the stars shrimp were playing;

In the sky ducks were roaming,

On the horizon beavers were turning.

The gold boats sank,

The silver boats sank,

The copper boats sank,

The iron boats and the tin boats sank.

Nienongluozuopo

Gathered all the gods to have a discussion:

Nienongsasaxie was sent,

Princess Luotaji was sent,

Gumuzheyiba was sent,

To deal with the flood.

Gumuzheyiba

Came up with an idea:

The water gate in the east was opened,

The water gate in the south was opened,

西方水门开,
北方水门开,
四方水门开,
大水还是淌不干。

他叫来白尾巴乌鸦:
"你去叫石蚌蹬开山口,
叫石蚌踢开水眼;
让洪水从山口流走,
让洪水从水眼淌完。"

洪水逐渐降落,
可是落水太慢。
涅侬撒萨歇,
罗塔纪姑娘,
古木折意巴,
一齐来巡察。

古木折意巴,
再派白尾巴乌鸦,
飞去喊太阳,
飞去喊月亮。

白尾巴乌鸦放声唤:

The water gate in the west was opened,
The water gate in the north was opened,
The water gates in the four direction were all opened,
But the flood did not drain.

He called in the white-tailed crow and told it:
"Go and ask the frogs to make mountain passes,
Go and ask the frogs to make water channels.
Let the flood flow out of the mountain passes,
Let the flood flow out of the water channels."

The flood level was getting lower,
But it was too slow.
Niunongsasaxie,
Princess Luotaji,
And Gumuzheyiba,
Came to inspect it together.

Gumuzheyiba
Asked the white-tailed crow
To go and call the sun for help,
To go and call the moon for help.

The white-tailed crow shouted loudly:

查姆 // Chamu

"太阳快出来!
月亮快出来!"
月亮和太阳,
不理睬白尾巴乌鸦。

罗塔纪姑娘,
再派白老鹰,
叫它飞到太阳落处,
叫它飞到月亮落处,
把日月衔起来。
白尾巴老鹰最听话,
它把太阳衔出来,
它把月亮衔出来。

他们派太阳来晒水,
他们派月亮来烤河川。
太阳火辣辣,
月亮亮闪闪,
晒了九天九夜,
烤了九天九夜,
洪水落了九天九夜。
洪水落了三尺,
洪水落了九千丈,
葫芦也落了九千丈;

Book One

"Sun, please show up quickly!
Moon, please show up quickly!"
The moon and the sun
Ignored the white-tailed crow.

Princess Luotaji
Sent a white eagle
To where the sun set,
To where the moon set,
To pick them up with its beak.
The white-tailed eagle was the most obedient,
It picked up the sun,
It picked up the moon.

They sent the sun over to dry the flood,
They sent the moon over to drain the rivers.
The sun was scorching,
The moon was shining,
The sun beat down for nine days and nights,
The moon shone for nine days and nights,
The flood receded for nine days and nights,
The flood level fell three feet.
When the flood level fell nine thousand feet,
And the gourd also fell nine thousand feet,

现出了山峦，
露出了平原，
树尖冒新芽，
地上草再生。

岩边有三蓬树：
一蓬细篾树，
一蓬尖刀树，
一蓬小竹树。
三种树相交错，
三种树紧相连，
三种树搭成棚，
三种树遮住天。

葫芦往下落，
落在竹树间，
树枝竹梢缠紧葫芦，
把葫芦拴在岩边。

二、找葫芦

洪水洗净了大地，
洪水洗净了万物。
涅侬撒萨歇，

Book One

Mountains emerged,
Plains appeared,
New leaves grew on the trees,
New grass grew on the ground.

On a cliff were three clumps of bamboo:
One clump was thin bamboo,
One clump was sharp bamboo,
One clump was small bamboo.
The three clumps intertwined one another,
The three clumps grew close together,
The three clumps of bamboo formed a shed,
The three clumps of bamboo provided shade.

The gourd continued to fall
And dropped into the bamboo clumps.
It was tangled in bamboo leaves
And tree branches on the cliff.

II. Looking for the Gourd

The flood cleaned the earth,
The flood cleaned everything.
Nienongsasaxie

为找大葫芦,

寻人传人烟,

又来到了人间。

涅侬撒萨歇啊,

从高山找到平坝,

从平坝找上高山。

迎面遇上老土蜂,

笑着把话问:

"土蜂、土蜂你到处飞,

略见着大葫芦?

葫芦上还糊有黄蜡,

两兄妹就藏在里面。"

土蜂忙回答:

"没有见着大葫芦,

没有见到两兄妹。

要是见着嘛,

糊葫芦的黄蜡,

我早把它吃完。"

涅侬撒萨歇,

怒火涌心间:

"土蜂的心肠坏,

上部
Book One

Came to the world again

To look for the big gourd,

To pass on their gene through blood.

Nienongsasaxie

Searched from mountain to plain,

Sought from plain to mountain.

He ran into a wasp

And asked with a smile,

"Dear wasp, you often fly around.

Have you seen a big gourd?

Beeswax is the seal on the gourd,

A brother and sister are hiding inside."

The wasp answered:

"I've never seen the gourd,

I've never seen the brother and sister.

If I'd seen it,

I would have eaten up

The beeswax on it."

Nienongsasaxie

Was filled with anger:

"You wasps are nasty,

查姆 // Chamu

土蜂的嘴太馋。
要叫后代人,
用火烧死你!"
从此以后嘎,
彝家见了老土蜂,
用火烧它才心甘。

涅侬撒萨歇,
继续往前看,
迎面来了葫芦包①:
"葫芦包啊葫芦包,
你到处飞舞,
咯见个大葫芦?
咯见着两兄妹?"

葫芦包嗡嗡叫:
"没有见着大葫芦,
也没见到两兄妹。
要是见着嘛,
我要叮死他俩,
饱饱吃一餐。"

涅侬撒萨歇,

---
① 葫芦包:一种野蜂的名称。

Book One

You are greedy.

I'll ask future human beings

To burn you to death!"

Since then,

When the Yi people see wasps,

They can't help burning them with fire.

Nienongsasaxie

Went on searching.

He ran into a Hulubao①:

"Dear Hulubao,

As you dance around,

Have you ever seen a big gourd,

With a brother and sister inside?"

The Hulubao hummed:

"I've never seen the big gourd,

Nor the brother and sister inside.

If I ever saw them,

I'd have stung them,

And eaten them."

Nienongsasaxie

---

① Hulubao: a wild bee.

气得冒火烟：
"狠心的小东西，
心肠这么坏。
后代只配头朝下，
吊死才心甘。"
从此以后嘞，
葫芦包的子孙，
个个的头朝下悬。

涅侬撒萨歇，
继续往前看，
迎面来了小老鼠：
"老鼠、老鼠你到处钻，
略见着大葫芦？
葫芦里面有水，
葫芦里面有粮，
葫芦里面有两兄妹。"

小老鼠唧唧叫：
"没有见着大葫芦，
也没见到两兄妹。
要是见到了，
葫芦里的粮食，
我早把它吃完。"

Was furious:

"You, cruel bee,

You, evil bee.

I'll be happy to see your children

Hang upside down."

From then on,

Hulubao's descendants

All fly with their heads downward.

Nienongsasaxie

Went on,

And bumped into a small rat:

"Dear rat, you always run around.

Have you seen a big gourd?

There is water inside,

There is rice inside,

There is a brother and sister inside."

The small rat squeaked:

"I've never seen the big gourd,

Nor the brother and sister inside.

If I'd seen the gourd,

The rice in the gourd

Would have served as my food."

涅侬撒萨歇,
气得眼瞪圆:
"贪嘴的小东西,
数你讨人嫌!
后代人见了你,
人人揍你才喜欢。"
从此以后嘞,
老鼠一出现,
人人喊打不迟延。

涅侬撒萨歇,
继续往前赶,
迎面遇上小绿雀:
"小绿雀啊小绿雀,
你成天到处飞,
喀见着大葫芦,
喀见着两兄妹?"

小绿雀点头忙回答:
"没有见着大葫芦,
没有见着两兄妹。
要是见到了,
我找粮食给他们吃。"

Book One

Nienongsasaxie

Stared at it angrily:

"You greedy thing,

How annoying!

When future people see you,

They will beat you."

Ever since then,

Whenever rats show up,

They will be beaten.

Nienongsasaxie

Went on with his search.

He ran into a green finch:

"Dear finch,

You fly everywhere.

Have you ever seen a big gourd,

With a brother and sister inside?"

The green finch answered:

"I've never seen the big gourd,

Nor the brother and sister inside.

If I'd seen them,

I'd have found rice for them."

涅侬撒萨歇，
听了很喜欢：
"巧嘴的小绿雀，
你的心肠好，
庄稼熟了你先尝。"
从此以后嘞，
世上小绿雀，
田里新谷它先尝。

涅侬撒萨歇，
继续往前走，
迎面遇着老喜鹊：
"喜鹊啊喜鹊，
你成天到处飞，
喀见着个大葫芦，
喀见着兄妹俩？"

喜鹊喳喳叫，
"没有见着大葫芦，
没有见着兄妹俩。
要是见着嘛，
早就飞来把喜讯传。"

上部
Book One

Nienongsasaxie

Was very happy to hear that:

"How smart you are,

How kind-hearted you are,

You deserve to taste new rice from now on."

From then on,

Finches became the first

To taste new rice in the fields.

Nienongsasaxie

Walked on,

And ran into an old magpie:

"Dear magpie,

You fly around.

Have you seen a big gourd,

With a brother and sister inside?"

The magpie chirped:

"I've never seen the gourd,

Nor the brother and sister inside.

If I'd seen the gourd,

I'd have spread the good news around."

涅侬撒萨歇,
听了心里甜:
"好心的喜鹊呀,
今后请你住屋前。
客人来了你早知道,
时时听见你把喜讯传。"
从此以后嘿,
喜鹊房前来做窝,
站在枝头唱得欢。

涅侬撒萨歇,
继续往前走,
迎面来了小蜜蜂:
"小蜜蜂啊小蜜蜂,
你一生勤劳不偷闲;
你采百花到山间,
你喀见着个大葫芦,
你喀见着两兄妹?"

小蜜蜂嗡嗡唱:
"我见到了大葫芦,
我见到了两兄妹。
在东边高山上,
有座白岩山;

Book One

Nienongsasaxie

Felt happy at hearing this:

"Kind-hearted magpie,

You will be invited to live under the eaves.

You will know the coming of guests,

And be the one spreading good news."

Since then,

Magpies make nests under the eaves

And sing merrily in the branches.

Nienongsasaxie

Moved on.

He bumped into a honeybee.

"Dear honeybee,

You are never lazy and always hardworking;

You've been busy collecting nectar in the mountains.

Have you seen a big gourd,

With a brother and sister inside?"

The little bee hummed:

"I've seen the big gourd,

I'v seen the brother and sister inside.

On the high mountain in the east,

There is a white rocky peak,

白岩山边三蓬树，
一蓬细篾树，
一蓬小竹树，
一蓬尖刀树，
三种枝叶紧相连，
三种枝叶遮住天，
大葫芦就挂在枝头间。"

涅侬撒萨歇，
听罢笑开颜：
"辛勤的小蜜蜂，
世上百花任你采，
四季鲜花你先尝。
鲜花酿蜜香又甜，
人类子孙喂养你，
请你住进屋里面。"
从此以后嘿，
百花丛中的小蜜蜂，
人人见了都喜欢。

三、配　亲

涅侬撒萨歇，
找到了大葫芦，

Where there are three clusters of bamboo.

One cluster is slim bamboo,

The second is small bamboo,

The third is sharp bamboo,

Their branches and leaves are intertwined,

Blocking out the sky altogether.

The big gourd hangs in the branches and leaves. "

Nienongsasaxie

Beamed happily:

"Hard-working honeybee,

You will collect nectar as much as you wish,

You will taste fresh flowers as much as you like.

Honey made from nectar is fragrant and sweet.

Human beings will take care of you,

And invite you to live with them."

Afterwards,

The humming honeybees in flowers

Are loved by human beings.

Ⅲ. Marriage

Nienongsasaxie

Found the big gourd.

打葫芦口,
走出阿朴独姆两兄妹。

洪水已经退了,
大地一片荒寂。
百里无草木,
千里无鸟兽,
万里无人烟。

哥哥看了焦虑,
妹妹看了哭泣:
"家中鸡没有,
家中狗没有;
独有我兄妹,
咋个做人家?"
涅侬撒萨歇,
指点阿朴独姆:
"要让世上有人烟,
你们兄妹做夫妻。"

兄妹听了心中急,
兄妹怎能做夫妻?!

涅侬撒萨歇,

Out of it came
Apudumu and his sister.

The flood had receded,
The land looked deserted.
Within a hundred miles no grass or trees could be found,
Within a thousand miles no birds or animals could be sighted,
Within ten thousand miles no signs of human life could be seen.

The brother worried,
The sister sobbed:
"There are neither chickens
Nor dogs in the house,
But the two of us.
How can we make a family?"
Nienongsasaxie
Gave advice to Apudumu:
"If you want more people in the world,
You two must get married."

The brother and sister were troubled,
How can brother and sister be married?!

Nienongsasaxie

查姆 // Chamu

想了个好主意：
"兄妹能否做夫妻，
你们滚东西试一试。"

他拿来了簸箕，
又拿来了筛子，
交给兄妹俩：
"两件东西分离；
你们不做夫妻；
两件东西合拢，
你们就做夫妻。"

哥哥拿筛子上南山，
妹妹拿簸箕上北坡；
簸箕、筛子同时滚，
滚到箐底合一起。
妹妹看了低下头，
哥哥看了不出气①。

涅侬撒萨歇说：
"簸箕、筛子合一起，
兄妹能够做夫妻！"

---

① 不出气：不说话。

Hit upon an idea:
"To decide whether this is acceptable,
You can try rolling things."

He brought a dustpan
And a winnowing pan,
And gave them to the brother and sister:
"If the two things do not come together,
You won't get married;
If the two things come together,
You will get married."

The brother went to the southern mountain with the winnowing pan,
And the sister went to the northern slope with the dustpan;
The winnowing pan and the dustpan rolled down simultaneously,
And joined each other at the bottom of the valley.
The sister lowered her head,
The brother did not say a word.

Nienongsasaxie said:
"The dustpan and the winnowing pan came together,
The brother and sister can be husband and wife!"

阿朴独姆兄妹说：
"碰巧滚一块，
兄妹不能做夫妻。"

涅侬撒萨歇，
搬来一盘磨。
哥抬上扇去东山，
妹背下扇去西山，
两扇一齐滚下坡，
滚到箐底合一起。

涅侬撒萨歇说：
"石磨合在一起，
兄妹能够做夫妻。"

阿朴独姆回答：
"碰巧滚在一起，
还是不能做夫妻。"

涅侬撒萨歇，
取来针和线，
哥哥拿丝线站河头，
妹妹拿花针去河尾，
针线同时丢进河里，

Brother Apudumu and his sister said:

"It was just a coincidence.

Brother and sister should not get married."

Nienongsasaxie

Brought a stone grinder.

The brother went to the east mountain with the upper part,

The sister went to the west mountain with the lower part.

They let go of the two parts at the same time,

Again the two parts came together at the bottom.

Nienongsasaxie said:

"The stone mill came together,

So the brother and sister can get married."

Apudumu answered:

"It's still a coincidence,

We should not get married."

Nienongsasaxie

Brought a needle and thread,

The brother stood at one end of the river with the thread,

The sister stood at the other end of the river with the needle.

They threw the thread and the needle into the river at the same time,

冲到河滩看仔细，
丝线穿进花针里。

涅侬撒萨歇，
拍手笑嘻嘻：
"三件东西试三次，
三次相合在一起，
水顺沟流道理在，
你俩应当做夫妻。"

阿朴独姆兄妹俩，
羞得把头低，
无法再推辞，
只好答应做夫妻。

四、民族的来源

阿朴独姆兄妹成亲后，
生下三十六个小娃娃。
十八棵青冈树①，
十八朵马缨花，
他们两眼横着生，
他们都是小哑巴。

---

① 青冈树：指男孩。下句的马缨花，指女孩。

Book One

They rushed to the river beach to check,
The thread was right in the needle eye.

Nienongsasaxie
Clapped his hands and laughed:
"Now that we have tried three times,
Each time they fit each other fine.
Just like water should follow its way,
You should be husband and wife."

Apudumu and his sister
Lowered their heads shyly.
They could refuse no more,
And agreed to become a couple.

IV. Origin of Ethnic Groups

After Apudumu and his sister got married,
They gave birth to thirty-six kids.
Eighteen were oak trees[①],
And eighteen were rhododendron flowers.
All of them had two horizontal eyes,
Yet they were all mute.

---

① Oak trees: referring to boys. Rhododendron flowers in the following line stand for girls.

查姆 // Chamu

天天围在火塘边,
只是烤火不会说话。

涅侬撒萨歇,
想出办法医哑巴。
叫爹妈砍来竹子,
放在火塘里烧炸。
只听竹子叭叭响,
这个叫"阿嗞嗞",
那个叫"阿喳喳",
有的叫"啊呀呀"……
哑巴从此会说话。

一个抢锄头往东跑,
一个抢扁担往西跑,
三十六个好儿女,
各走一方分了家。

"阿嗞嗞"是彝语,
成了今天的彝家;
"阿喳喳"是哈尼语,
哈尼的祖先就是他;
"啊呀呀"是汉语,
他成了后来的汉家。

Book One

They sat around the hearth all day,
Without a word to say.

Nienongsasaxie
Came up with a cure.
He asked the parents to bring bamboo,
And burn them in the fire.
The bamboo made cracking sounds,
Then some kids was shouting "Azizi",
Others were shouting "Azhazha",
Still others were shouting "Ayaya"…
The mute kids could all speak from that time on.

One kid snatched a hoe and ran eastward,
Another grabbed a shoulder pole and ran westward.
The thirty-six children
Settled down in different places.

"Azizi" was the Yi language.
The people speaking it formed the Yi people;
"Azhazha" was the Hani language.
The people speaking it formed the Hani people;
"Ayaya" is the Chinese language,
The people speaking it formed the Han people.

查姆 // Chamu

抢锄头的是彝族，
抢扁担的是傣家；
彝族山头烧火地，
傣家挑担住平坝。
从此各人为一族，
三十六族分天下；
三十六族常来往，
和睦相处是一家。

世上有了人烟，
世上分了民族。
他们要生存繁衍，
他们要认识事物。
他们怎样开创历史，
他们又怎样创造万物？
彝家的兄弟啊，
请听后面的根谱。

Book One

The one with the hoe became the father of the Yi people;

The one with the shoulder pole became the father of the Dai people.

The Yi people went to the mountain and practiced slash and burn;

The Dai people went to the plain.

Every group formed a nationality,

The thirty-six nationalities divided the world;

The thirty-six nationalities got on well.

They were as close as one family.

Now there were human beings in the world,

There were different nationalities.

They wanted to survive and thrive,

They wanted to learn things.

How did they make history?

How did they create everything?

Dear Yi people,

Please listen to the following genealogy.

下部
Book Two

查姆 // Chamu

第一章　麻和棉

一、种　麻

大江边住着的白彝人,
是阿朴独姆的后裔,
房子多得像蜂窝,
人多得像蚂蚁,
就是没有衣裳穿,
大家心头都很着急。

歇索的三个儿子,
想出了个主意:
弯刀拿在手中,
斧子别在腰里,
去到大山头,
砍树种旱地。

斧子砍大树,
弯刀砍小树,

下部
Book Two

Canto 1 Flax and Cotton

I. Flax Planting

The Baiyi people lived along the big river.
They were the descendants of Apudumu.
Their houses were as crowded as beehives.
The population was as large as colonies of ants.
But they did not have clothes to wear.
They were all very worried about that.

Three of Xiesuo's sons
Came up with an idea.
With machetes in their hands,
With axes on their waists,
They went into the mountains and
Cut trees for farming on the dry land.

They cut down big trees with axes.
They cut down small trees with machetes.

查姆 // Chamu

木渣四方溅，
就像蝴蝶飞舞。
一连砍三天，
砍完一座山。
地上烧大火，
火焰冲上天。
三天火不熄，
烧了九座山，
遍地是草灰，
山头黑一片。

歇索的三个儿子，
回到了家中，
问爹妈和哥嫂，
要种什么庄稼？
阿爹说："要撒油菜籽。"
阿妈说："要撒芝麻籽。"
阿哥阿嫂说："要撒大麻籽。"
歇索的三个儿子，
阿爹的话要听，
阿妈的话有理，
阿哥阿嫂的话也可取。

公鸡不叫就起来，

Book Two

The bits of wood were flying,

Just like flying butterflies.

They kept cutting for three days.

They finally deforested the whole mountain.

They burnt the land.

The glare of the fire lit up the sky.

The fire kept burning for three days.

The vegetation of nine mountains was completely burnt out.

Plant ashes were everywhere.

The mountains had darkened tops.

The three sons of Xiesuo

Came back home.

They asked their parents, the eldest brother and his wife:

"What crops shall we plant?"

Father said: "Rapeseed."

Mother said: "Sesame seed."

The eldest brother and his wife said: "Flax seed."

For the three sons of Xiesuo,

Father's words were practical,

Mother's words were reasonable,

The eldest brother and his wife's words were acceptable.

They got up before the cock crowed.

查姆 // Chamu

大哥挑水，
大嫂煮米，
鸡叫忙吃饭，
带上荞粑粑和工具，
太阳一出就上山，
山头撒油菜籽，
山腰撒芝麻籽，
山下撒大麻籽。

过了两个月，
爹妈叫哥嫂去看地，
哥嫂叫三兄弟去看地，
歇索的三个儿子，
来到地边上，
大麻长得房子高，
油菜开花遍地黄，
芝麻开花飘白絮。

又过了三个月，
大麻秆长得白又直，
油菜籽结得压弯秆，
芝麻籽结满枝。

阿爹割油菜，

The eldest brother carried the water.

His wife cooked the rice.

They had breakfast in a hurry when the cock crowed.

They brought barley cakes and farming tools.

They got to the mountains as the sun rose.

They sowed rapeseed over the top of the mountain.

They sowed sesame seed on the mountainside.

They sowed flax seed at the foot of the mountain.

Two months later,

Their parents asked the eldest brother and his wife

To check on the fields,

But they asked the three younger brothers to do it instead.

They came to look at the fields.

The flax grew as tall as a house.

The yellow flowers of rape bloomed everywhere.

The white flowers of sesame waved like tassels.

Three months more,

Flax stems grew white and straight.

Rape stems were weighed down by fresh seeds.

Sesame stems were full of sesame seeds.

Father harvested rapeseed.

查姆 // Chamu

阿妈割芝麻,
阿嫂割大麻,
收割庄稼心欢喜。

歇索的家里,
菜籽堆满一屋子,
芝麻堆满一屋子,
大麻堆满一屋子。
爹妈望着笑眯眯,
哥嫂望着笑嘻嘻。

阿哥白天剥麻皮,
阿嫂夜晚把麻搓细,
绩成麻线织成布,
全家穿上麻布衣。

阿爹白天剥麻皮,
阿妈晚上搓麻绳,
搓成麻绳织成网,
拿着江上去打鱼。

剩下的拿去街上卖,
卖得金银买家具。
江边白彝人,

Mother harvested sesame.

The eldest brother's wife harvested flax.

It was a great joy to harvest crops.

At the home of Xiesuo,

One room was filled with rapeseeds.

One room was filled with sesame seeds.

One room was filled with flax.

Parents looked at them with big smiles.

The eldest brother and his wife had great joys.

The eldest brother peeled the flax in the daytime.

His wife made thread in the evening.

Flax thread was made into linen cloth.

The whole family got dressed in linen clothes.

Father peeled the flax in the daytime.

Mother twisted it to make twine.

Twine was made into nets.

Nets were used for fishing in rivers.

The rest of flax was sold in the market.

Furniture was bought with the gold and silver.

The Baiyi people along rivers

日子过得还富裕。
穿上自织麻布衣，
织网种地又猎渔。

二、种　棉

麻布衣裳有了，
棉布衣服还没有。

哪个来种棉？
哪个来纺纱？
哪个来织布？
哪个来染花？

歇索的三个儿子，
晚上搓麻绳，
白天上山支扣子。
山头支副扣子，
山腰支副扣架，
山脚支副扣架。

过了三天去查看：
山顶那一扣，
小羚羊挣断扣索；

Book Two

Lived a prosperous life.

They had home-made linen clothes to wear.

They had farming tools and fishing nets.

II. Cotton Planting

There was linen clothing,

But not cotton clothing.

Who could plant cotton?

Who could do cotton spinning?

Who could do cotton weaving?

Who could do cotton cloth dyeing?

The three sons of Xiesuo

Twisted twine in the evening

And went hunting in the mountains during the daytime.

They laid a trap at the top of the mountain.

They laid a trap at the mountainside.

They laid a trap at the foot of the mountain.

Three days later, they went back to have a look:

The one at the top of the mountain

Failed to catch a muntjac.

山腰那一扣,
麝子没勒着;
山脚那一扣,
没有扣住山鸡脚。

三兄弟想了想:
菜籽抓一把,
麻籽抓一把,
芝麻抓一把。
山顶扣子下面撒菜籽,
山腰扣子下面撒芝麻,
山脚扣子下面撒麻籽。

又过两天去查看:
山顶那一扣,
没扣着小羚羊;
山腰那一扣,
没扣着麝子;
山脚那一扣,
扣着只大孔雀。

孔雀很好看:
头上红三道,
身穿五彩衣,

Book Two

The one on the mountainside

Failed to catch a musk deer.

The one at the foot of the mountain

Failed to catch a pheasant.

The three brothers thought for a while.

They took a handful of rapeseeds.

They took a handful of flax seeds.

They took a handful of sesame seeds.

They put rapeseeds under the trap at the top of the mountain.

They put sesame seeds under the trap at mountainside.

They put flax seeds under the trap at the foot of the mountain.

They went back in two days:

The one at the top of the mountain

Still failed to catch a muntjac.

The one on the mountainside

Still failed to catch a musk deer.

The one at the foot of the mountain

Finally caught a big peacock.

It was a beautiful peacock,

With three red stripes on its head,

Colorful feathers everywhere,

查姆 // Chamu

身上绿三道,
翅膀铜钱花,
尾巴像蝴蝶,
开屏像彩霞。

歇索的三个儿子,
把孔雀带回家。
爹妈见了问:
"这个是什么鸟啊?
头上三道红。"
哥嫂见了问:
"这个是什么鸟啊?
身上三道花。"
姑娘见了问:
"到底是什么鸟啊?
尾巴像蝴蝶,
翅膀铜钱花。"

阿哥忙回答:
"山中最美的是马缨花,
鸟中最美的是花孔雀,
今天是吉祥的孔雀到我家。"

歇索的三个儿子,

Three green stripes on its body,

A coin-shaped pattern on its wings and

A butterfly-like pattern on its tail.

It was an enchanting cloud when it fanned out.

The three sons of Xiesuo

Brought the peacock home.

Their parents asked:

"What kind of bird is it?

There are three red stripes on its head. "

The eldest brother and his wife asked:

"What kind of bird is it?

There are three green stripes on its body. "

Their daughter asked:

"What on earth kind of bird is it?

It has a tail with a butterfly-like pattern.

It has wings with a coin-shaped pattern."

The three brothers answered:

"The most amazing flower in the mountain is the rhododendron flower.

The most beautiful bird in the forest is the peacock.

Today, the auspicious peacock comes to our home."

The three sons of Xiesuo

剖开孔雀头，
不见脑浆只有三颗棉花籽；
剖开孔雀心，
没有心血只有三颗棉花籽；
破开孔雀骨，
没有骨髓只有三颗棉花籽；
取出九颗棉花籽，
交给阿爹阿妈。
阿爹拿着喜欢，
阿妈看着高兴，
把它藏在柜旮旯。

布谷鸟枝头叫，
撒种的时候到啦！
爹妈从柜里取出棉籽，
土掌房上晒一下。

歇索的三个儿子，
来到地里种棉花。
阿嫂撒种子，
阿哥弄犁耙，
清明撒下种，

Opened the head of the peacock.

There was no brain but three cotton seeds inside.

They opened the heart of the peacock.

There was no blood but three cotton seeds.

They broke the bones of the peacock.

There was no marrow but three cotton seeds.

They took out the nine cotton seeds,

And gave them to their parents.

Their father was delighted to have the cotton seeds.

Mother was happy to see the cotton seeds.

They kept them safely in the corner of the closet.

Cuckoos started to chirp.

It was the time for sowing.

Parents got the cotton seeds from the closet.

They dried them on the flat roof of the earthen hut.

The three sons of Xiesuo

Went to the field to plant cottons.

The eldest brother's wife scattered the seeds.

The eldest brother worked with a plough.

The cotton seeds were sown on the day of Qingming[①].

[①] Qingming: one of the 24 solar terms for agriculture in the Chinese lunar calendar. It usually falls on Apr. 5th. —Translator's note

谷雨抽嫩芽。

过了一个月,
哥嫂去瞧棉花,
棉苗绿油油,
一棵棉花五个杈。

又过三个月,
棉苗长得又高又大,
棉桃压枝头,
棉田白花花。

歇索一家人,
忙着收棉花。
棉花堆满一屋,
满屋都是花。
歇索家会种棉,
消息传遍天下。
乡亲们赶来看,
十人看了九人夸。

歇索老爹问大家:

The cotton seeds started to sprout on the day of Guyu①.

One month later,

The eldest brother and his wife went to have a look.

The cotton seedlings were all green.

Each cotton seedling had five twigs.

In three months more,

The cotton seedlings grew tall and strong.

The twigs were weighed down by huge cotton bolls.

The cotton fields were completely white.

The whole family of Xiesuo

Were busy harvesting cotton,

Which filled their house

Like full of white flowers.

The family of Xiesuo could plant cotton.

The news was known by everyone.

The villagers all came to see.

Nine out of ten sang high praise for them.

Father Xiesuo asked everyone:

---

① Guyu: one of the 24 solar terms for agriculture in the Chinese lunar calendar. It usually falls on Apr. 19th. —Translator's note

"哪个会纺纱？
哪个会织布？"
德白西回答：
"我会纺纱。"
哈若西回答：
"我会织布。"
歇索一家听了欢喜，
乡亲们听了高兴，
有的吹起芦笙，
有的吹起唢呐，
就请德白西纺纱，
就请哈若西织布。

德白西白天纺纱，
哈若西晚上织布。
德白西把棉花纺成了纱，
哈若西用纱线织成纱帕。

棉布是织出来了，
缺少光泽颜色差。
歇索的三个儿子，
到街上买染料。

Book Two

"Who can do cotton spinning?

Who can do cotton weaving?"

Debaixi answered:

"I can do cotton spinning."

Haruoxi answered:

"I can do cotton weaving."

The Xiesuos were excited to hear that.

All the villagers were delighted to hear that.

Some of them blew the lusheng[①].

Others played the suona[②].

Debaixi was invited to do cotton spinning.

Haruoxi was invited to do cotton weaving.

Debaixi did cotton spinning in the daytime.

Haruoxi did cotton weaving in the evening.

Debaixi made cotton yarn by spinning.

Haruoxi used cotton yarn to weave cloth.

The cotton cloth was done.

But there was no color or shine.

The three sons of Xiesuo

Went to the market to buy dyes.

---

① Lusheng: a traditional wind instrument made of reed pipes. —Translator's note
② Suona: a traditional wind instrument similar to a trumpet. —Translator's note

他们从街头找到街尾，
染料满街挂。
红黑黄蓝样样有，
绚丽似彩霞。
各样颜料买三斤，
急急忙忙拿回家。

德白西染布，
哈若西配画。
各色布匹染出了，
泉水洗布布光滑。

从那个时候起，
江边白彝人，
身穿棉布衣，
头包黑纱帕。

They walked through the street,
Which was rich in various dyes,
Red, black, yellow and blue,
Resembling colorful clouds at dusk.
They bought three kilos of each color
And went home in a hurry.

Debaixi dyed the cotton cloth.
Haruoxi designed the patterns.
They made the cloth colorful.
They smoothed it in spring water.

From then on,
The Baiyi people along rivers
Were dressed in cotton clothes
And wore black cotton turbans.

查姆 // Chamu

第二章　绸和缎

泽梗子地方,
有了满五月姑娘,
她第一个知道采桑,
她第一个开始养蚕。

姑娘背着背箩,
每天都爬上高山,
找寻各种叶片片,
采摘回家喂蚕。

走到山头上,
采来绿松针;
走到梁子上,
采来渣拉叶片;
走到大河边,
采来锥栗叶尖。
三种叶子给蚕吃,
蚕儿不吃也不闻。

下部
Book Two

Canto 2　Silk and Brocade

In the town of Zegengzi
Lived a girl named Manwuyue.
She was the first to pick mulberry leaves.
She was the first to know how to raise silk worms.

Every day, she climbed the mountain
With a basket on her back.
She picked the various leaves she found,
And brought them home to feed silk worms.

She reached the top of the mountain,
And picked green pine needles.
She climbed to the mountain ridge,
And picked Zhala leaves.
She went to the riverside,
And picked tender chestnut leaves.
She fed the silk worms with these leaves,
But they neither ate nor smelled them.

查姆 // Chamu

人不吃饭不能活，
蚕不吃食就会死。
满五月姑娘，
又背着箩筐，
四面八方找蚕的饭。

坝中割青草，
河边割藤蔓，
山头采鲜花，
三样东西来喂蚕，
蚕儿还是不吃，
蚕儿还是不咽。

人不吃饭不能活，
蚕不吃食怎吐丝？
满五月姑娘，
再次背背箩上山，
四面八方找蚕的饭。

门前掐来菜叶，
路边扯来柿叶，
山上采来桑叶，
三种叶子倒成三堆，

下部
Book Two

People couldn't live without food.

Silk worms couldn't live without proper leaves.

The girl Manwuyue

Went out again with her basket,

To look for leaves for her silk worms.

She cut the grass on the flatland,

Cut the vines on the riverside,

And picked flowers in the mountains.

She then fed the silk worms with them.

But they neither tasted them

Nor swallowed them.

People couldn't live without food.

Silk worms couldn't produce silk without eating.

The girl Manwuyue

Went out again with her basket,

To look for leaves for her silk worms.

She picked vegetable leaves in front of her house.

She picked persimmon leaves by the roadside.

She picked mulberry leaves from the mountains.

She put the three different leaves in three piles,

三种叶子给蚕吃。
菜叶蚕不闻,
柿叶蚕不挨,
桑叶蚕儿吃得喳喳响。
满五月姑娘见了喜欢,
天天采桑叶,
天天仔细看。

蚕儿吃了桑叶长得快,
蚕儿吐丝啦!
白蚕吐白丝,
黑蚕吐黑丝,
绿蚕吐绿丝,
红蚕吐红丝,
黄蚕吐黄丝。
五样颜色的蚕,
吐出五种丝。

收得蚕丝怎么缫?
收得蚕丝怎么办?
列贵挨姑娘说:
"蚕丝我会缫。"

她有四个好伙伴:

And fed them to the silkworms.
They neither smelled the vegetables
Nor touched the persimmon leaves.
But they crunched all the mulberry leaves.
The girl Manwuyue was thrilled to see that.
She picked mulberry leaves every day.
She watched silk worms crunch them every day.

The silk worms grew fast after eating the mulberry leaves.
They started to produce silk!
The white silk worms produced white silk.
The black silk worms produced black silk.
The green silk worms produced green silk.
The red silk worms produced red silk.
The yellow silk worms produced yellow silk.
Silk worms of five colors
Produced five types of silk.

How to reel silk from cocoons?
How to use the silk?
A girl named Liegui'ai said:
"I can reel silk from cocoons."

She had four good friends:

查姆 // Chamu

一个峨阿拉姑娘,
一个峨奇俐姑娘,
一个峨夺白姑娘,
一个峨佐作姑娘,
她们四个会缫丝。

白丝缫成堆,
缫得八千团;
黑丝缫成堆,
缫得九千团;
绿丝缫成堆,
缫得八千团;
红丝缫成堆,
缫得九千团;
黄丝缫成堆,
缫得八千团;
缫得一百二十堆,
堆满九屋十八院。

列贵挨姑娘真能干,
领头缫丝织绸缎。
六个姑娘十二只手,
织的绸缎数不完。

A girl named E'ala,

A girl named Eqili,

A girl named Eduobai,

A girl named Ezuozuo.

They all could reel silk from the cocoons.

The white silk was reeled and piled up.

There were eight thousand reels.

The black silk was reeled and piled up.

There were nine thousand reels.

The green silk was reeled and piled up.

There were eight thousand reels.

The red silk was reeled and piled up.

There were nine thousand reels.

The yellow silk was reeled and piled up.

There were eight thousand reels.

The total was one hundred and twenty piles.

They filled up nine rooms and eighteen yards.

Liegui'ai was a competent girl.

She led other girls to reel silk and weave brocade.

Six girls with twelve hands

Wove countless brocade.

绸缎织出来了，
还得染绸缎，
不染无色彩，
不染不好看。
哪个找染料？
哪个会染绸缎？

歇索的三个儿子，
都是找虎的好汉。
他们三个齐声说：
"要找颜料不用愁，
要染绸缎不费难。"

他们背着金弓银弩，
他们带上金箭银箭，
领着黑狗白狗，
天天打虎撵山。

他们四处寻找，
找遍了七十七条箐，
寻遍了九十九道湾，
搜遍了一百二十个峰峦，
才找到了老虎的脚印。

Bolts of brocade were woven,
But they must be dyed,
Or they would be colorless
And unattractive.
Who could find dyes?
Who could dye the brocade?

The three sons of Xiesuo
Were all good tiger-hunters.
They said together:
"Don't worry about finding the dyes.
Don't worry about dyeing the brocade."

They took gold bows and silver crossbows.
They brought gold arrows and silver arrows.
They had black hounds and white hounds.
They went hunting in the mountains.

They searched everywhere for prey.
Having searched seventy-seven valleys,
Having searched ninety-nine vales,
Having searched one hundred and twenty hills,
They finally found the footprints of a tiger.

歇索的三个儿子，
放出黑狗白狗，
拉满金弓银弩，
搭上金箭银箭，
一个山顶滚石头，
两个挡住虎路口。

老虎出来了，
金弓放一箭，
从老虎头上飞过；
银弩放一箭，
从老虎脚下飞过；
金弓银弩一齐放，
箭穿老虎的肋骨，
射中老虎的心肝。
大哥二哥抬老虎，
三弟背弩箭。
老虎抬到家，
用金刀剥下老虎皮，
用银刀剖开虎心肝，
挖出护心血，
取出胸中胆，
送给姑娘们染绸缎。

The three sons of Xiesuo

Released the black hounds and white hounds.

They drew their bows back to the full,

Ready to shoot.

One rolled a huge rock from the mountain top.

The other two blocked the tiger's way out.

The tiger came out.

The gold bow released an arrow,

Which flew over the tiger's head.

The silver bow released an arrow,

Which flew under the tiger's paws.

Two bows released arrows at the same time.

One arrow pierced through the tiger's ribs.

The other one hit the tiger's heart.

Two elder brothers carried the tiger.

The youngest brother carried the bows and arrows.

They took the tiger home,

Skinned it with a gold knife,

Opened its heart with a silver knife,

Took out its blood and gall-bladder,

And gave them to the girls

For brocade dyeing.

六个姑娘接过护心血,
六个姑娘收下老虎胆,
她们晚上织绸缎,
白天染绸缎,
绸缎染得红彤彤,
绸缎染得光闪闪。

染了又再画,
样样画齐全。
画上月亮和太阳,
画上大地和蓝天。
星宿也画上,
画上片片云彩;
风雨也画上,
画出锦绣山川;
老虎豹子也画上,
马鹿麂子画齐全;
山鸡箐鸡也画上,
红雀绿雀山鹰喜鹊画得展翅飞云端;
庄稼树木也画上,
还画上牲畜和人烟……

染也染过了,
画也画过了,

Book Two

Six girls took the tiger's blood.

Six girls took the tiger's gall-bladder.

They wove brocade in the evening,

They dyed brocade in the daytime.

The dyed brocade was reddish.

The dyed brocade was sparkling.

Pattern-designing came after dyeing.

Everything was drawn on the brocades,

The moon and the sun,

Vast land and blue sky,

Stars and planets,

Colorful clouds,

Wind and rain,

Splendid mountains and rivers,

Tigers and leopards,

Deer and muntjacs,

Pheasants and roosters were in the patterns.

Red birds, green birds, hawks and magpies were flying in the clouds.

Crops and trees,

And livestock and people…

After dyeing and patterning,

The brocade must be

还要洗来还要漂,
漂过洗过才美观。

漂洗绸缎没有水,
六个姑娘找水源。
她们走过八十个坝子,
经过八十八座高山;
山下有龙潭,
潭里流清泉,
清泉水好染绸缎。

六个姑娘来挑水,
六个姑娘挑六担;
三担水洗绸,
三挑水漂缎,
绸缎洗得像月亮,
绸缎染得颜色鲜。

绸缎漂好哪里晒?
拿到城里去晒干。
挑着绸缎回到泽梗子,
四道城门大大开,
人出人进像蚂蚁一般。

Washed and cleaned
To really look glamorous.

There was no water to wash the brocade.
The six girls looked for the water source.
They passed through eighty flatlands
And climbed over eighty-eight mountains.
At the foot of one mountain there was a pond,
Where clear springs bubbled out,
And the water was good for washing the brocade.

The six girls carried home
Twelve buckets of water with shoulder poles.
Three buckets were used for silk washing.
Three buckets were used for brocade cleaning.
The brocade was washed as clean as the moon.
The brocade was dyed shiny and bright.

Where would the washed brocade be dried?
They were to be dried in the town.
The girls went back to Zegengzi with the brocade.
The four gates of the town were completely opened.
Folks came and went like colonies of ants.

城墙上晒红绸子,
城楼上晒黄缎子,
城墙上一片红,
城楼上一片黄。

皇帝见了动心,
都府见了红眼,
县官见了笑成泥一团。
姑娘做成的绸缎,
他们要先拿,
他们要先用,
他们要先穿。

后代的子孙呵,
穿上绸和缎,
莫忘了打虎的兄弟,
莫忘了满五月姑娘采桑养蚕。

下部
Book Two

The red silk was dried on the town walls.

The yellow brocade was dried on the town towers.

The town walls were all red.

The town towers were all yellow.

The emperor was interested.

The prefect was jealous.

The county magistrate was wild with joy.

The brocade made by the girls

Were taken by them first,

Used by them first,

And worn by them first.

People of the future!

When you are dressed in silk and brocade,

Don't forget the brothers who hunted the tiger,

Or the girl who picked mulberry leaves for the silk worms.

查姆 // Chamu

第三章　金银铜铁锡

泽梗子地方，
黑夺方地方，
有一家两兄弟，
哥哥叫萨阿勒，
弟弟叫西阿德，
阿勒阿德两兄弟，
他们认得藏金银的地方，
他们知道藏铜铁的地方。

三星还没有落，
两兄弟就起床，
鸡叫忙煮饭，
天亮上山冈，
去找金银铜铁锡。
他们走啊走，
走到可叶山上。
山脚细细瞧，
山腰细细找，

Book Two

Canto 3　Gold, Silver, Copper, Iron and Tin

In the town of Zegengzi,
In the town of Heiduofang,
There lived two brothers.
The elder brother was named Sa Ale.
The younger brother was named Xi Ade.
But they were simply called Ale and Ade.
They knew where to find gold ore and silver ore.
They knew where to spot iron ore and copper ore.

When the stars were still in the sky,
The two brothers got up.
They cooked breakfast when the cock started to crow.
They climbed to the mountain ridges at dawn,
Looking for gold, silver, copper, iron and tin.
They walked and walked.
They reached Keye Mountain.
They searched the foot of the mountain,
Examined the mountainside,

查姆 // Chamu

看见一大棵金树,
树干黄澄澄,
树叶放金光,
树花晶晶亮。
阿勒阿德两兄弟,
心中喜洋洋。
两人齐声说:
"挖开金山采金矿。"

他们继续往前走,
走到峨俫山梁。
山脚细细瞧,
山腰细细找,
看见一大棵银树,
树叶白生生,
树花亮堂堂。
阿勒阿德两兄弟,
脸上笑眯眯。
两人齐声说:
"挖开银山采银矿。"

他们继续往前走,
走到过俫山梁。
山脚细细瞧,

And finally saw a big gold tree.
The trunk was bright yellow.
The leaves were glittering gold.
The blossoms were sparkling.
The two brothers
Were extraordinarily excited.
They said together:
"Let's dig into the gold mountain to mine gold ore."

They walked on,
Arriving at the ridge of Eluo Mountain.
They searched the foot of the mountain,
Examined the mountainside.
And finally saw a big silver tree.
The leaves were pure white.
The blossoms were glistening.
The two brothers
Were extremely happy.
They said together:
"Let's dig into the silver mountain to mine silver ore."

They moved on,
Arriving at the ridge of Guoluo Mountain.
They searched the foot of the mountain,

山腰细细找,

看见一棵铜树明晃晃。

满树红彤彤,

树叶亮堂堂。

阿勒阿德兄弟俩,

心头乐滋滋。

两人齐声说:

"挖开铜山采铜矿。"

他们继续往前走,

走到纳铁山梁。

山脚细细看,

山腰细细找,

看见一棵大铁树,

树干黑黝黝,

树叶嫩汪汪。

阿勒阿德兄弟俩,

心头好喜欢。

两人齐声说:

"挖开铁山采铁矿。"

他们继续往前走,

走到过梗山梁。

山脚细细瞧,

Examined the mountainside,

And finally saw a big copper tree.

The whole tree was bright reddish.

The leaves were shining.

The two brothers

Were completely delighted.

They said together:

"Let's dig into the copper mountain to mine copper ore."

They went on,

Arriving at the ridge of Natie Mountain.

They searched the foot of the mountain,

Examined the mountainside,

And finally saw a big iron tree.

The trunk was black.

The leaves were tender.

The two brothers

Were particularly pleased.

They said together:

"Let's dig into the iron mountain to mine iron ore."

They went on,

Arriving at the ridge of Guogeng Mountain.

They searched the foot of the mountain,

山腰细细找,
看见一棵大锡树,
锡树白花花,
树叶放白光。
阿勒阿德兄弟俩,
嘴上笑眯眯。
两人齐声说:
"挖开锡山采锡矿。"

兄弟俩走遍五座大山,
找到了埋在山中的宝藏。
他们要挖出金石头,
挖出银石头,
挖出铜石头,
挖出铁石头,
挖出锡石头,
挖出五种矿。

金银铜铁锡,
五种矿石五个样,
可惜没有水洗,
矿石难放光。

阿勒阿德两兄弟,

Examined the mountainside,

And finally saw a big tin tree.

The whole tree was brilliantly milky.

The leaves were emitting white light.

The two brothers

Were smiling with joy.

They said together:

"Let's dig into the tin mountain to mine tin ore."

They searched all over five mountains,

And found the hidden treasures.

They wanted to mine the gold ore,

The silver ore,

The copper ore,

The iron ore,

And the tin ore.

They would mine the five types of ores.

Gold, silver, copper, iron and tin

Were different metal ore.

Without water to wash them, though,

The metals couldn't shine.

The two brothers

到处去找水。
走到文依地方,
找到一股水;
走到赛铁梗邹地方,
找到两股水;
走到塔罗莫科地方,
找到三股水;
走到靖宁梗邹地方,
找到四股水;
走到多别鸟井地方,
找到五股水;
走到买迷峨井地方,
找到六股水;
走到文依梭泽地方,
找到七股水;
走到梁子黑龙水地方,
找到八股水。

两兄弟找到了水,
一齐动手洗矿石。
银石洗得白生生,
金石洗得亮堂堂,
铁石洗得黑黝黝,
铜石洗得明晃晃,

Looked for water everywhere.

When they arrived at a place called Wenyi,

They found a stream.

When they arrived at a place called Saitiegengzou,

They found two streams.

When they arrived at a place called Taluomoke,

They found three streams.

When they arrived at a place called Jinninggengzou,

They found four streams.

When they arrived at a place called Duobieniaojing,

They found five streams.

When they arrived at a place called Maimi'ejing,

They found six streams.

When they arrived at a place called Wenyisuoze,

They found seven streams.

When they arrived at a place called Lianziheilongshui,

They found eight streams.

Having found water,

They started to wash the ores together.

The silver ore was washed pure white.

The gold ore was washed bright and glittering.

The iron ore was washed glossy black.

The copper ore was washed shiny clean.

锡石洗得白云样,
样样矿石都放光。

矿石找到了,
矿石洗净了。
可惜没有木炭,
还是不能炼矿。

阿勒阿德两兄弟,
去到峨罗山上,
松树砍了三架山,
柏树砍了十八凹,
栗树砍了九条箐,
他们挖成窑子,
木炭烧出来了。

阿勒阿德两兄弟,
半山砍棵攀枝花树,
做个大风箱。
用土墼砌个大炉子,
木炭放在正中央,
手拉风箱炉火旺。

阿勒去烧火,

Book Two

The tin ore was washed cloudy white.
All the ores were sparkling.

Metal ores were found.
Metal ores were washed.
However, without charcoal,
The metals couldn't be refined.

The two brothers
Went to Eluo Mountain.
They cut down pines on three hills.
They cut down cypresses in eighteen gullies.
They cut down chestnut trees in nine vales.
They dug and built a kiln,
And made charcoal by burning the wood.

Ale and Ade, as they were called,
Cut down a red cotton tree on the slope,
And made a big bellows.
They used clay bricks to make a big oven,
Put charcoal in the center,
And pumped the bellow's handle to keep the fire burning.

Ale put the charcoal in the fire,

查姆 // Chamu

阿德扯风箱,
火光像闪电,
风箱如雷响。
兄弟两个笑眯眯,
流着汗珠炼出矿。

哪个来打金锭银锭?
哪个来打金银首饰?
哪个来打锄头镰刀?
哪个来打茶壶铃铛?

泽梗子地方,
黑夺方地方,
梗郭的三个儿子,
他们白天炼金,
他们晚上铸银,
金块炼成金锭,
银块铸成银锭。
他们白天打金,
他们晚上打银。
金子打成金首饰,
银子打成银首饰。
他们白天炼铜,
他们晚上打铁,

While Ade pushed the bellows handle.
The flames were like lightning.
The bellows was thundering.
The two brothers smiled with great joy.
They refined the metals by sweating a lot.

Who could cast the gold ingots and silver ingots?
Who could make the gold and silver jewelry?
Who could make hoes and sickles?
Who could make pots and bells?

In the town of Zegengzi,
In the town of Heiduofang,
The three sons of Gengguo
Refined gold in the daytime,
And silver in the evening,
Turning chunks of gold into gold ingots,
And chunks of silver into silver ingots.
They hammered gold in the daytime.
They struck silver in the evening.
Gold was made into gold jewelry.
Silver was made into silver jewelry.
They smelted copper in the daytime.
They struck iron in the evening.

查姆 // Chamu

用铜铁做成铜壶铜盆,
用铁打成锄头镰刀,
用锡做成各种用具。

泽梗子地方,
黑夺方地方,
是出金银的地方,
是使用金银的地方。
十斤和五斤,
十两和五两,
不足一斤不使,
不足一两不用。

泽梗子地方嫁囡,
使金使银很平常;
黑夺方地方讨亲,
使金使银很大方;
世上死了人,
使金用银办丧葬。
泽梗子地方的小姑娘,
戴金戴银闪闪亮;
黑夺方地方的小伙子,
戴金戴银人夸奖,
在他们身上,

Book Two

Copper was made into pots and basins.

Iron was made into hoes and sickles.

Tin was made into various tools.

The town of Zegengzi and

The town of Heiduofang

Were rich in gold and silver,

And well known for using gold and silver too.

They had weight units of ten *jin*, five *jin*,

Ten *liang* and five *liang*.

They did not use

Other units to measure gold and silver.

Gold and silver are commonly used

When the daughters of families in Zegengzi got married.

The families in Heiduofang were generous

In using gold and silver when their sons got married.

When people passed away,

Gold and silver were used for funerals.

Young girls in Zegengzi

Wore shining gold and sparkling silver.

Young boys in Heiduofang

Were admired for wearing gold and silver.

On their bodies,

金子银子亮晃晃,
金银首饰响叮当。

梗郭的三个儿子,
造出工具千万样。
锄头镰刀有了,
用具什物有了,
世上需要的东西,
样样都造出来了。

Gold and silver were glistening.

Metal jewelry was jingling.

The three sons of Gengguo

Made a variety of tools.

There were hoes and sickles.

There were instruments and implements.

The articles to meet the needs of daily life

Were all produced.

查姆 // Chamu

第四章　纸和笔

纸用什么造成的？
笔用什么造成的？
纸用树皮造成的，
笔用竹子麝毛造成的。
什么人先造纸？
什么人先造笔？
这是很古的事情，
样样都有来历。

歇索大山上，
歇阿乌最先说：
"我们要写字，
没有纸和笔。"

歇索的三个儿子，
跟着歇阿乌，
白天去找做纸的树皮，
晚上去找做笔的竹枝。

Canto 4   Paper and Brush Pen

What is paper made of?

What are brush pens made of?

Paper is made from tree bark.

Brush pens are made of bamboo and the hairs of the musk deer.

Who was the pioneer to make paper?

Who was the pioneer to make brush pens?

This is a very old story.

Everything has its origin.

In Xiesuo Mountain,

Xie'awu was the first to say:

"We want to write,

But we have neither paper nor brush pens."

The three sons of Xiesuo

Followed Xie'awu.

They looked for tree bark in the daytime.

They looked for bamboo sticks in the evening.

找到东方去,
遇着老绿龙。
歇阿乌请求它:
"东方是你管理,
这里算你强,
有没有竹枝?
有没有造纸的树皮?"
老绿龙回答说:
"东方绿城是我管理,
我没有竹子,
我没有造纸的树皮。"

找到南方去,
遇着老白龙。
歇阿乌请求它:
"南方是你管理,
这里算你有本事,
有没有竹子?
有没有树皮?"
老白龙回答说:
"南方白城是我的属地,
竹子我没有,
树皮我没有。"

Book Two

They went to the east
And came across the old green dragon,
Whom Xie'awu begged:
"You are in charge of the east.
You are the strongest one here.
Do you have bamboo sticks?
Do you have tree bark for paper-making?"
The old green dragon answered:
"I am in charge of the Green City in the east,
But I have neither bamboo
Nor tree bark for paper-making."

They went to the south
And came across the old white dragon,
Whom Xie'awu begged:
"You are in charge of the south.
You are the most competent here.
Do you have bamboo sticks?
Do you have tree bark for paper-making?"
The old white dragon answered:
"I dominate the White City in the south,
But I have neither bamboo
Nor tree bark for paper-making."

找到北方去,
遇着老黑龙。
歇阿乌请求它:
"北方属你管理,
这里数你第一,
有没有竹子?
有没有树皮?"
老黑龙回答说:
"北方黑城是我管理,
我没有竹子,
我没有树皮。"

找到西方去,
遇着老红龙。
歇阿乌请求它:
"西方属你管理,
西方数你第一,
有没有竹子?
有没有树皮?"
老红龙回答说:
"西方红城是我管理,
我没有竹子,
我没有树皮。"

下部
Book Two

They went to the north

And came across the old black dragon,

Whom Xie'awu begged:

"You are in charge of the north.

You are the most powerful here.

Do you have bamboo sticks?

Do you have tree bark for paper-making?"

The old black dragon answered:

"I control the Black City in the north,

But I have neither bamboo

Nor tree bark for paper-making."

They went to the west

And came across the old red dragon,

Whom Xie'awu begged:

"You are in charge of the west.

You are the most influential here.

Do you have bamboo sticks?

Do you have tree bark for paper-making?"

The old red dragon answered:

"I rule the Red City in the west,

But I have neither bamboo

Nor tree bark for paper-making."

查姆 // Chamu

歇索的三个儿子,
跟着歇阿乌,
带上金弓银弩,
领着猎狗,
钻进老箐里。

歇阿乌吹牛角,
猎狗汪汪叫。
撵出一对豹子,
穿的铜钱花衣,
撵出一对老虎,
穿着镰刀花衣。

歇阿乌搭上银箭,
射到半天空,
云彩被打散。
再放第二箭,
射到山肚里,
山崩塌一半。
射不中虎豹,
箭头也不见。

歇索的三个儿子,

下部
Book Two

The three sons of Xiesuo

Followed Xie'awu.

They brought gold bows and silver crossbows,

And went into the deep valleys

With their hounds.

Xie'awu blew the ox horn.

The hounds started to bark.

Two leopards ran out,

With coin-like spots on their fur.

Two tigers rushed out,

With sickle-like stripes on their bodies.

Xie'awu took out the silver arrow.

He shot into the sky,

And dispersed the clouds.

He shot another arrow

To the center of the mountain,

And half of the mountain collapsed.

But he missed the leopards and tigers,

And lost his arrows.

The three sons of Xiesuo

跟着歇阿乌，
继续往前走。
猎狗进箐，
牛角吹响，
出来一对马鹿，
穿的红彤彤，
出来一对野猪，
穿的黑黝黝。

歇阿乌拉起银弩，
射到半空中，
天空红一半。
再一箭射到地上，
地炸起一块，
冒起一股尘烟。

箭头不见了，
没射中野猪、马鹿，
他们继续往前赶，
心中起疑团。

牛角吹响了，
猎狗钻进深山，
撵出黑漆漆的一对山驴，

Book Two

Followed Xie'awu.

They kept moving on.

Their hounds went into the valley.

Their ox horn was blown.

Two deer came out

With reddish fur.

Two wild boars came out

With blackish fur.

Xie'awu drew the silver crossbow,

And shot into the sky.

Half of the sky turned rosy.

He then shot into the ground,

Breaking off a chunk of earth

And sending dust into the air.

He lost his arrows again,

And missed the wild boars and deer.

They kept moving on

With confusion in minds.

The ox horn was blown.

Hounds went into the mountain,

And drove out two black donkeys

查姆 // Chamu

撵出灰仆仆的一对岩羊。

歇阿乌搭上银箭,

箭飞上天,

天白一片。

又放一箭,

箭钻进树,

三棵大树被射断。

射不中山驴、岩羊,

难不倒歇阿乌。

又把猎狗放进孟吾大山①,

两边喊哦嚯!

牛角嘟嘟响。

撵出一只麝子。

他们搭上银箭,

箭飞上天,

降下一阵猛雨;

又放一箭,

箭钻进地,

地冒一股水。

雨停河水涨,

淌出一支金箭来。

---

① 孟吾大山:地名。

Book Two

And two grey blue sheep.

Xie'awu put the silver arrow on the bow.

The arrow flew into the sky,

Which turned bright.

He shot another arrow.

It flew into the woods,

And split three big trees.

The failure to kill the donkeys and blue sheep

Didn't daunt Xie'awu.

They let the hounds go into Mengwu Mountain①,

Shouted from the valley rim,

Blew their horns loudly,

And drove out a musk deer.

They shot a silver arrow.

It flew into the sky

And a heavy downpour of rain came.

They shot one more arrow.

It went into the ground

And a spring rushed out.

When the rain stopped, the river swelled

And a gold arrow was drifting in the river.

---

① Mengwu Mountain: the name of a place.

歇阿乌拉起银弩，
歇阿乌搭上金箭，
射到麝子的肋巴里，
麝子倒毙。

歇索的三个儿子，
把麝子抬回家里，
歇阿乌剖开麝头，
麝头没有脑浆，
却有二颗竹子种，
有三颗纸树籽。
挖开麝心，
麝子心中没有血，
却有三颗竹子种，
有三颗纸树籽。
敲开麝骨头，
不见有骨髓，
却有三颗竹子种，
有三颗纸树籽。

歇索的三个儿子，
跟着歇阿乌，
砍出三块地，
放火来烧地，

Xie'awu drew the silver crossbow,

Fitted the gold arrow to the string,

And shot it into the ribs of the musk deer.

The musk deer fell down and died.

The three sons of Xiesuo

Carried the musk deer back home.

Xie'awu opened the head of the musk deer.

There was no brain in it

But three seeds of bamboo and

Three seeds of the tree for paper-making.

He opened the heart of the musk deer.

There was no blood in it

But three seeds of bamboo and

Three seeds of the tree for paper-making.

He opened the bones of the musk deer.

There was no marrow in them

But three seeds of bamboo and

Three seeds of the tree for paper-making.

The three sons of Xiesuo

Followed Xie'awu.

They got three pieces of land by slashing plants.

They burned the land for planting.

查姆 // Chamu

烧出草灰种纸树。

竹子种撒满山坡，
纸树籽撒在地里。
竹子绿茵茵，
纸树露白皮。

歇索的三个儿子，
跟着歇阿乌，
银刀别腰上，
砍回三捆竹子，
砍回三捆纸树，
砍倒三棵青冈树，
做成打纸棒，
背回一个大石滚，
用石滚来碾纸。

歇阿乌的阿妈，
白天打纸，
晚上打纸，
竹子做笔管，
麝毛做笔头，
做成纸和笔。

The ashes were used to plant trees for paper-making.

They scattered bamboo seeds over the hillside
And seeds of trees for paper-making in the fields.
Bamboo grew up with glossy green leaves.
Trees for paper-making grew up with white bark.

The three sons of Xiesuo
Followed Xie'awu.
They kept silver knives on their waists,
And cut three bundles of bamboo,
Three bundles of trees for paper-making,
And three oaks
To make hammers for smashing paper pulp.
They carried a huge round rock back home
For paper-pressing.

Xie'awu's mother
Smashed paper pulp in the daytime,
And pressed paper in the evening.
Bamboo was made into the handles of brush pens.
The musk deer fur was made into the tips of brush pens.
Paper and brush pens finally came into being.

查姆 // Chamu

笔有了,
纸也有了,
一百二十个老师,
不分热天和冷天,
不管风季和雨季,
让彝家子子孙孙读书写字。

Book Two

Now there were brush pens.

Now there was paper too.

One hundred and twenty teachers

Taught Yi Children reading and writing,

No matter whether it was hot or cold,

Windy or rainy.

第五章　书

泽梗子地方,

有三条河谷,

有三座高山,

住着三个伙伴。

一个叫赛季考叶莫,

一个叫俫佐赛叶勒,

一个叫多俫勒文莫。

三人齐撒种,

树种撒得多,

遍地树花数不清。

阿朴独姆西嘛,

树木名字不晓得,

山川名字不会分……

黑夺方地方,

山梁有三个,

大坝有三个。

山梁上有竹子绿茵茵,

Book Two

Canto 5   Books

In the town of Zegengzi,
There were three river valleys.
There were three high mountains.
There lived three friends.
One was named Saijikaoyemo,
One was named Luozuosaiyele,
One was named Duoluolewenmuo.
The three friends did sowing together.
Many seeds were sown and countless trees
And flowers came out everywhere.
There was a man named Apudumuxi,
Who knew neither the names of trees
Nor the names of mountains and rivers…

In the town of Heiduofang,
There were three mountain ridges.
There were three flatlands.
The mountain ridges were covered with green bamboo.

查姆 // Chamu

山梁上的藤子满坡生。
坝子的青草绿又嫩,
坝子里的海水明如镜。
阿朴独姆西嘛,
竹子藤子不晓得,
大海小海不会分,
年月节令也分不清。

涅侬撒萨歇,
百事都关心,
把人间的难事,
找罗阿玛询问。

龙王罗阿玛,
昼夜画图写书文。
天地日月画出来,
草木风雨画出来,
粮食种子画出来,
马鹿野兽画出来,
男人女人画出来……
阿朴独姆西也画出来,
世上万物一齐画出来。

画成万物十二册,

Book Two

The mountain ridges were full of woody vines.
The flatlands were covered with tender grass.
The flatlands were dotted with mirror-like ponds.
The man Apudumuxi
Could not tell bamboo from rattan,
Nor big ponds from small ones.
He did not even know years, months or seasons.

Nienongsasaxie
Cared about everything.
He asked Luo'ama for solutions
To all human problems.

Luo'ama, the Dragon Queen,
Spent all his days and all his nights drawing and writing.
The sky, the earth, the sun and the moon were drawn.
The grass, the wood, the wind and the rain were drawn.
Crops and seeds were drawn.
Deer and other beasts were drawn.
Men and women were drawn...
Apudumuxi was drawn too.
Everything in the world was drawn.

He made twelve volumes of drawings.

写成字书十二本。
有本有篇又有行，
样样画得清，
事理写得明。

龙王罗阿玛，
向黑夺方丢下画图来，
向泽梗子丢下书文来，
把图画和书文送给人间。

阿朴独姆西拾起字书，
翻了又翻，
吟了又吟。
白天学书上的画，
夜晚学书上的文。
书上的字学会了，
书上的道理懂得了，
万事万物也会分了。

天气冷一回，
就是一年啰，
年大十三月，
年小十二月；
月亮圆一回，

He wrote twelve books.

There were volumes, chapters and lines.

Everything was drawn clearly.

Every idea was explained clearly.

Luo'ama, the Dragon Queen,

Dropped the drawings off at Heiduofang

And the books at Zegengzi,

Bestowing both to the human world.

Apudumuxi picked up the books,

Turned them page by page,

And read again and again.

He studied the drawings in the daytime.

He learnt the writings in the evening.

He learnt all the words in the books.

He understood all the ideas.

He could tell one thing from another.

When the weather turns cold,

The end of a year is near.

There are thirteen months in a leap year

And twelve months in a common year.

When the moon becomes full,

就是一月啰，
月大三十天，
月小二十九天；
十四、十五月亮圆，
十六、十七月更明；
年月大小书上有，
日子长短书上写得清，
天干地支书上写得明。

阿朴独姆西，
喊来儿子和姑娘，
告诉书上的道理：
莫忘老古根，
莫忘老书文。

这些书是祖先拾得的，
这些书是祖先写下的，
它是阿朴独姆西一代一代传下来的。
没有这些书，
万物名字咋记清？

你说罗阿玛大，
我说涅侬倮佐坡更大，
天地和万物，

Book Two

It is another month.

There are thirty days in a longer month

And twenty nine days in a shorter month.

The moon becomes full on the 14^(th) and the 15^(th),

But it is brighter on the 16^(th) and 17^(th).

The length of years and months and days

Are clearly written in the books.

So are the Heavenly Stems and Earthly Branches.

Apudumuxi

Asked his sons and daughters to come over.

He told them the principles from the books:

Never forget their old roots,

Never forget the old books.

The old books were collected by their ancestors.

The old books were written by their ancestors.

They have been passed down by Apudumuxi.

Without these books,

How could the names of things be remembered?

You say Luo'ama is great.

But I say Nielongluozuopo is greater.

The sky, the earth and everything in the world

查姆 // Chamu

是他们创造的。
他们的功劳载书上,
他们的功劳万古存。

他说天地大,
我说天地不算大,
天地的名字自己不会取,
天地的名字要人来取,
要是没有书,
名字谁来记?

你说日月星宿大,
我说日月星宿大,
日月星宿不算大,
日月星宿的名字自己不会取,
日月星宿的名字人来取,
取了名字记书上。
要是没有书,
名字不会有。

你说天王地王大,
我说天王地王大,
天王管着日月星辰,
地王管着世上万物。

下部
Book Two

Were created by them.

Their achievements are recorded in the books.

Their achievements are remembered forever.

He says the sky and the earth are great.

I say they are not.

They couldn't name themselves.

They were named by people.

What if there were no books?

Who could name them?

You say the sun, the moon and the stars are great.

I say the sun, the moon and the stars are great.

Actually, they are not.

They couldn't name themselves.

They were named by people.

Their names were recorded in books.

What if there were no books?

They would have no names.

You say the King of Heaven and the King of Earth are great.

I say the King of Heaven and the King of Earth are great.

The King of Heaven controls the sun, the moon and the stars.

The King of Earth rules everything in the world.

查姆 // Chamu

天王地王不算大，
天王地王的名字自己不会取，
天王地王的名字人来取，
取了名字记书上。
要是没有书，
名字不会有。

你说独眼睛人大，
我说独眼睛人大；
你说直眼睛人大，
我说直眼睛人大；
你说横眼睛人大，
我说横眼睛人大；
独眼睛人的时代没有书，
独眼睛人的名字自己不会取；
直眼睛人的时代没有书，
直眼睛人的名字自己不会取；
横眼睛人的时代没有书，
横眼睛人的名字自己不会取。
独眼睛人的名字，
直眼睛人的名字，
横眼睛人的名字，
都是后代人来取，
他们还是不算大。

下部
Book Two

However, they are not that great.

They couldn't name themselves.

They were named by people.

Their names were recorded in books.

What if there were no books?

They would have no names.

You say the one-eyed people were great.

I say the one-eyed people were great.

You say the vertical-eyed people were great.

I say the vertical-eyed people were great.

You say the horizontal-eyed people were great.

I say the horizontal-eyed people were great.

But there was no book in the era of the one-eyed people.

They couldn't name themselves.

There was no book in the era of the vertical-eyed people.

They couldn't name themselves.

There was no book in the era of the horizontal-eyed people.

They couldn't name themselves.

The one-eyed people,

The vertical-eyed people,

And the horizontal-eyed people

Were all named by later generations.

They were not that great.

查姆 // Chamu

我说天上的娑罗树大,
娑罗树长在月亮里,
娑罗树千年不会死。
娑罗树不算大,
娑罗树的名字自己不会取,
娑罗树的名字人来取,
取了名字记书上。
要是没有书,
名字不会有。

你说粮食树木大,
要是没有粮食,
阿朴独姆西活不成;
要是没有树木,
鸟兽怎安寝?
粮食树木不算大,
粮食树木不会自己取个名,
粮食树木的名字人来取,
取了名字记书上。
要是没有书,
粮食树木难区分。

你说鸟兽大,

下部
Book Two

I say the heavenly sala tree is great.

The sala tree grows in the moon,

And will never die.

However, the sala tree is not that great.

It couldn't name itself,

But was named by people.

Its name was recorded in books.

What if there were no books?

It would have no name.

You say crops and trees are great.

Without crops,

Apudumuxi couldn't survive.

Without trees,

How could birds and animals sleep peacefully?

However, crops and trees are not that great.

They couldn't name themselves.

Crops and trees were named by people.

Their names were recorded in books.

What if there were no books?

It would be impossible to tell them apart.

You say birds and beasts are great.

鸟兽会唱各样音。
九十架山梁上，
老虎豹子叫，
马鹿麝子鸣；
深沟老箐里，
山鸡野鸡吟；
河边岩子上，
野兔岩羊叫不停；
荆棘刺蓬里，
黑蛇绿蛇哼。
鸟兽不算大，
鸟兽的名字不会自己分，
鸟兽的名字人来取，
取了名字记书上。
书上有鸟兽的名字，
从此鸟兽有大名。

你说山梁子大，
他说山梁子高入云，
三十六架山梁子上，
密布葱葱老林，
山梁上万花红遍，
山梁上果实累累，
山梁子不为大，

They can make diverse sounds.

On ninety mountain ridges,

Tigers and leopards are roaring,

Deer and musk deer are calling.

In the deep valleys,

Roosters and pheasants are crowing.

On the rocks of river banks,

Hares and blue sheep are bleating.

In the bramble bushes,

Black snakes and green snakes are hissing.

However, birds and beasts are not that great.

They couldn't name themselves.

They were named by people.

Their names were recorded in books.

With names in books,

They have been known by everyone.

You say mountain ridges are great.

He says mountain ridges touch the clouds.

Thirty-six mountain ridges are covered

With dense and old jungle,

Colorful flowers,

And juicy fruit.

However, mountain ridges are not that great.

山梁子不会自己取个名,
山梁子的名字人来取,
山梁子名字记书上,
从此山梁子天下闻名。

你说坝子大,
他说坝子宽无垠。
三十六个大坝子,
流水潺潺绕坝心;
三十六个大海子,
海里白浪尽翻滚。
老鹰天上转,
白鹤水面飞,
野鸭水中扇翅膀,
大鱼小鱼闪金鳞,
水獭想吃鱼,
常常徘徊在海滨。
坝子、海子不算大,
坝子、海子的名字自己不会取,
坝子、海子的名字人来取,
坝子、海子的名字记书上,
从此坝子、海子有大名。

你说江河大,

下部
Book Two

They couldn't name themselves.

They were named by people.

Their names were recorded in books.

They have been known by everyone.

You say flatlands are great.

He says flatlands are extraordinarily vast.

In thirty-six flatlands,

Clear streams are running in the center.

In thirty-six lakes,

Waves are rolling,

Hawks are circling above them,

White cranes are flying over them,

Mallards are fluttering in the water,

Fish of different size are glittering,

And beavers are lingering along the banks,

Because they are greedy for the fish.

However, flatlands and lakes are not that great.

They couldn't name themselves.

They were named by people.

Their names were recorded in books.

From then on, they have been known by everyone.

You say rivers are great.

他说江河深。
三十六条江,
条条宽又长,
条条江水归大海,
条条江水流不尽。
江水不算大,
江水的名字自己不会取,
江水的名字人来取,
江水名字记书上,
从此大江大河有个名。

你说十二样礼节大,
他说十二样礼节难分清。
学会磕头作揖第一样,
分清日月星宿能辨时辰,
学会处人办事第三样,
尊敬爹妈道理明,
分清一年四季第五样,
婚丧嫁娶众遵循,
喜客爱朋彝家礼,
说话恭谨人相亲,
读书求学寻常事,

He says rivers are deep.

Thirty-six rivers,

All are wide and long.

All the rivers are running into the oceans,

With endless water.

However, rivers are not that great.

They couldn't name themselves.

They were named by people.

Their names were recorded in books.

Since then, they have been known by everyone.

You say the twelve kinds of etiquette are great.

He says they are difficult to differentiate.

The first is to learn how to kowtow and zuoyi①.

Next is to know the sun, the moon and the stars and tell correct time.

The third is to learn to deal with people and matters.

Next is to know why and how to respect one's parents.

The fifth is to understand the four seasons in a year.

Next is to follow the traditions of weddings and funerals.

Next is to be hospitable and nice to friends and visitors.

Next is to talk with people politely and warm-heartedly.

Next is to keep learning as a necessity in one's life.

---

① Zuoyi: it means making a slight bow with hands folded in front. —Translator's note

十二样礼节记在心。
十二样礼节记书上,
规矩、礼节教子孙。

世上万物有字书,
世上万物有图画,
万物的名字罗阿玛写出来,
字书是阿朴独姆西传下来,
彝家的规矩是阿朴独姆西教出来。
假若没有阿朴独姆西,
字书谁过问?
假若没有字书,
彝家的道理谁传闻?

The twelve kinds of etiquette should be kept in mind.

They have been recorded in books,

And should be taught to one's descendants.

Everything has been recorded in books.

Everything has been drawn in pictures.

The name of everything was written by Luo'ama.

The books have been passed down by Apudumuxi.

The traditions have been taught by him, too.

What if there was no Apudumuxi?

Who would write the books?

Without the books,

Who could inherit the principles of the Yi people?

查姆 // Chamu

第六章　长生不老药

彝家学会开矿藏，

学会种麻粮，

学会织绸缎，

学会养猪羊。

有吃有穿不用愁，

只愁有病咋医治。

只愁有病不死嘛，

还要找寻长生不老药。

彝家有个老阿妈，

名叫拉兵也欧，

三年病魔缠身，

请来西波①叫魂。

祭神送鬼都搞过，

疾病还是不见好；

世上药草都吃遍，

---

① 西波：即贝玛，或朵觋。在缺医少药的旧社会，生产力低下，人有了病就请西波念经送鬼。西波识彝文，是彝族的知识分子。

Book Two

Canto 6   The Elixir

The Yi people had learned to mine ores,

To plant flax and other crops,

To weave silk and brocade,

And to raise pigs and goats.

They no longer worried about food and clothing.

They only worried about how to cure diseases.

As they didn't want to die from diseases,

They searched for elixir.

There was an old Yi lady,

Whose name was Labingye'ou.

She had suffered from a disease for three years.

A xibo① was sent for to call back her soul.

Sacrifice for gods and demons was also done.

But the sick lady was not getting better.

No medicinal herbs worked, either.

---

① Xibo: also known as beima or duoxi. They were the intellectuals in the Yi people. They were invited to chant spells to drive away evil spirits from sick people.

- 255 -

查姆 // Chamu

要吃长生不老药才会好。

哪个知道长生不老药?
这种药又到哪里找?
拉兵也欧的儿子,
也叫拉兵也欧。
他身披披毡,
头戴篾帽,
骑着马儿去求医,
找来神药救阿妈。

拉兵也欧啊,
翻过千座山,
渡过万条河,
四方都找遍,
问过老少和渔樵,
听说有一个姑娘,
名叫西说阿墨勒,
她认得长生不老药。
拉兵也欧跳下马,
去找西说阿墨勒。

消息传进皇宫里,
皇帝派儿子来抢药。

Book Two

Only the elixir could cure her.

Who knew about the elixir?
Where to find it?
Labingye'ou had a son,
Who was also named Labingye'ou.
He put on his felt cloak and bamboo hat,
And went out on his horse
To look for doctors and magical medicine
To save his mother.

Oh, Labingye'ou
Climbed over a thousand mountains,
And crossed a thousand rivers.
He looked everywhere, asking
Old and young, fishermen and woodcutters,
And was told that there was a girl
Named Xishuo'amole
Who knew about the elixir.
Labingye'ou got off his horse
To visit Xishuo'amole.

The news of elixir reached the royal court.
The emperor sent his son to get the elixir by force.

查姆 // Chamu

他们吹着唢呐,
他们敲着锣鼓,
扛着旗子带着兵,
要把长生不老药抢进宫廷。

他们审问西说阿墨勒:
"长生不老药在哪里?
快点交出来!
免挨棍棒打,
免挨坐监牢!
只要交出来,
金银任你抓,
绸缎任你挑!"

西说阿墨勒姑娘,
咬着牙齿叉着腰。
"我什么也没有,
我什么也不知道。"

皇帝的儿子,
等了三夜三朝。
用尽欺哄骇诈,
耍了无数花招,
西说阿墨勒姑娘,

Book Two

They blew suona.

They beat gongs.

They led troops and held flags,

Determined to take the elixir into the royal court.

They interrogated Xishuo'amole:

"Where is the elixir?

Hand it over to us quickly!

Or you'll be beaten with sticks,

Or even put into jail!

As long as you hand it over,

You can take as much gold and silver as you like,

And as much as silk and brocade as you want."

The girl Xishuo'amole

Clenched her teeth with arms akimbo:

"I have nothing.

I know nothing."

The son of the emperor

Waited for three days and three nights.

He tried every means of cheating and intimidating.

He played bunches of tricks.

But the girl Xishuo'amole

查姆 // Chamu

就是不交出长生不老药苗。

白树山头上,
有一个牧羊佬,
放着一群绵羊,
羊像白云飘。

牧羊佬晚上数羊,
一只大公羊不见了。
第二天清早,
三个牧羊人,
带着猎狗四处找,
走遍大山小箐,
寻遍深山林坳,
都没有把羊子找到。

三个牧羊人,
来到荒山坳。
看见公羊倒在大树旁,
原来公羊吃了草乌叶①,
嘴里吐白沫,
不动也不叫。

---

① 草乌:一种野生药材,毒性很大。

Book Two

Still refused to hand over the elixir.

On the top of the White-Tree Mountain
Lived an old shepherd.
He was pasturing a herd of sheep,
As white as drifting clouds in the sky.

The old shepherd counted his sheep in the evening,
And found a big ram missing.
The next morning,
Three shepherds looked for the ram
With the help of four hounds.
They searched all the big and small valleys.
They checked on the mountains and in the jungle.
But they failed to find the missing ram.

The three shepherds
Came to a desolate col.
They saw the ram lying next to a tree.
It was still and voiceless,
Foaming at the mouth,
Obviously poisoned by the aconitum[①] it ate.

---

① Aconitum: a kind of extremely poisonous medicinal herb.

三个牧羊人,
围着大公羊落泪,
围着大公羊伤悲。
西说阿墨勒姑娘,
突然来到荒山坳。
她拿出仙药敲敲羊头,
羊头抬起来了;
她用药敲敲羊脚,
羊脚动起来了;
她再用药敲敲羊身子,
羊就会跑会跳了。

牧羊人又喜又笑,
就向姑娘讨药苗:
"把你的仙药分给我们,
天上星星摘给你,
地上金银随你要。"

姑娘微微笑:
"你们要仙药不难,
回去拿东西来换:
我要白麂的牙齿,
我要世上最好的口弦。"

Book Two

The three shepherds
Surrounded the ram and shed sad tears.
The girl Xishuoa'mole
Came to the desolate col all of a sudden.
She took out the magical medicine
To pat the ram's head,
And the ram looked up.
She used it to pat the ram's hoofs,
Which started to move.
She used it to pat the ram's body,
And the ram could run and jump again.

The shepherd laughed in great joy.
He asked the girl for the medicine:
"If you share your medicine with us,
We'll pick up the stars in the sky for you,
And give you as much gold and silver as you want."

The girl smiled:
"It's easy for you to get the magical medicine.
Go back and bring things in exchange for it.
I want the teeth of the white musk deer.
I want the best jaw harp.

查姆 // Chamu

"口弦身边带得有,
白麝牙齿设法找。"
三个牧羊人告诉拉兵也欧,
忙把公羊往回吆。

拉兵也欧啊,
为了救活阿妈,
下决心去打白麝,
不怕山高路遥。

他领上十二只猎狗,
抬上十二张猎网,
天不亮就动身,
天黑还不歇脚。
走到大山上,
走到悬崖边,
走到大江畔,
走到小河旁,
走进老林里,
钻进草蓬中,
熬过了无数的白天黑夜,
不见麝子心里焦。

有一天走到山梁上,

Book Two

"We have the jaw harp with us,

But the teeth of the white musk deer cannot be found,"

The three shepherds told Labingye'ou,

And went back home with the ram.

Labingye'ou,

Anxious to save his mother,

Decided to hunt the white musk deer,

Despite high mountains and long distances.

He took with him twelve hounds

And twelve hunting nets.

He started his journey before dawn,

And didn't ever stop after dusk.

Climbing mountains,

Walking along cliff edges,

Going along river banks,

Walking along brooks,

Going into old jungles,

Getting through bushes,

He went through countless days and nights,

Extremely worried, as he saw no white musk deer.

He walked to a mountain ridge one day,

查姆 // Chamu

看见细沙路上两行脚印,
猎狗闻到麝子味,
对着山梁汪汪咬。
大狗堵中间,
小狗围四方。

只听草在响,
只见草在摇,
一对麝子跑出来,
张嘴露白牙,
抬头四处瞧。

拉兵也欧拉满弓,
一箭射中白麝腿,
白麝滚山腰。
麝肉喂大狗,
麝血喂小狗,
麝香官家要,
麝皮送给西波,
麝牙留着换药苗。

他解下身上的口弦,
他带上麝子的牙齿,
找到西说阿墨勒,

下部
Book Two

And saw two lines of footprints on a sandy track.

The hound smelled the musk deer.

They kept barking towards the mountain ridge.

The big hound guarded the middle exit.

The small hounds besieged the ridge on all sides.

The rustling of grass was heard.

The fluttering of grass was seen.

A pair of musk deer ran out of the grass,

Showing their white teeth

And looking around.

Labingye'ou drew back the bow to the full,

And hit a white musk deer on the leg.

The white musk deer rolled down to the mountainside.

The musk deer flesh was fed to the big coursers.

The musk deer blood was fed to the small hounds.

The musk deer gland was taken by the magistrate.

The musk deer fur was given to xibo.

The musk deer teeth were kept to barter for the elixir.

He went to see Xishuo'amole

And offered the jaw harp.

And the teeth of the white musk deer,

去换长生不老的药苗。

西说阿墨勒姑娘,
一手接口弦,
一手接麝牙,
睁大眼睛仔细瞧。
她告诉拉兵也欧:
"白山头上,
有棵三杈树,
树叶绿茵茵,
树枝分三杈,
树左挖三下,
就能挖到长生不老药苗。

"还要配上长虫、白麝胆,
配上绵羊山羊胆。
要细细地舂,
要透透地熬,
病人吃了就会好,
好人吃了长生不老。"

拉兵也欧啊,
把姑娘的话记牢。
药配好了,

In exchange for the seedling of the elixir.

The girl Xishuo'amole

Took the jaw harp in one hand

And the teeth in the other,

Examining them closely.

Then she told Labingye'ou:

"On the top of the White Mountain,

There is a tree with three branches.

Its leaves are bright green.

Each branch has three twigs.

Dig three times on the left of the tree,

And you'll find the seedling of the elixir.

It should be finely pounded,

And thoroughly stewed

With long worms and the gall-bladders

Of white musk deer, sheep and goats.

This medicine will restore health to any patients,

And turn healthy people into immortals."

Labingye'ou

Kept the girl's words in his mind.

When the ingredients for the medicine were ready,

又去问西说阿墨勒姑娘：
"药应该怎样舂？
药又应该怎样熬？"
西说阿墨勒姑娘说：
"你去打只老鹰来，
鹰头做杵臼，
鹰骨做杵棒，
翅膀来扫药，
鹰脚当药盅，
滚沸开水来熬药。"

拉兵也欧把药舂好，
煮药的水到哪里找？
无火怎样把药熬？
西说阿墨勒姑娘说：
"没有水莫着急，
没有火莫心焦，
我到龙王处借水，
我到家中找火苗。"

拉兵也欧啊，
样样东西都有啦，
到麻栎树底下，
烧火把药熬。

Book Two

He went to ask the girl Xishuo'amole:

"How do I pound the medicine?

How do I stew the medicine?"

The girl Xishuo'amole told him:

"Go hunt a hawk.

Use its head as the mortar,

Its bone as the pestle,

Its wings to sweep the medicine,

Its feet as the cups to drink the medicine from.

Stew the medicine in boiling water."

Labingye'ou pounded the medicine,

But where could he find water?

Where could he find fire?

The girl Xishuo'amole told him:

"Don't worry about water.

Don't get anxious about fire.

I'll borrow water from the Dragon Queen.

I'll get fire from my home."

Labingye'ou

Got everything ready now.

He went under an oak,

And made fire to stew the medicine.

查姆 // Chamu

药气熏上麻栎树,
从此一年换一次叶,
千年万载不会凋。
世上所有的树,
都被药气熏过,
不管雪打雨淋,
不管日晒风吹,
年年都换叶,
年年长新枝。

拉兵也欧把药煮,
就是没有搅药的东西,
折枝松桠来搅,
松树沾上药味,
万年长青永不凋。

药汤煮涨了,
忽然一阵风吹过,
药汤熏在杨柳上,
从此倒插杨柳,
插在哪里哪里会生苗。

拉兵也欧嘛,
把煮好的药端给阿妈吃,

下部
Book Two

The medicine vapor rose up to the oak.

Since then, that oak has stayed vigorous

For thousands of years by shedding its leaves annually.

All the trees on the earth,

Steamed by the medicine vapors,

Shed their old leaves every year

And grew new branches every year,

No matter in rain or snow,

No matter in sunshine or wind.

Labinye'ou was stewing the medicine.

But he needed something to stir it.

He picked a twig from a pine.

Nourished by the smell of the medicine,

The pine stayed evergreen for thousands of years.

When the medicine was boiling,

A breeze carried the vapor to the willows.

Since then,

Willow twigs could sprout,

Wherever they were planted.

Labingye'ou

Took the stewed medicine to his mother,

医好了阿妈的病,
阿妈就长生不老。
药罐里还剩点药汤,
请大家都来尝尝。

东方的人吃了,
东方的人永远不会死;
南方的人吃了,
南方的人永远不会死;
西方的人吃了,
西方的人永远不会死;
北方的人吃了,
北方的人永远不会死;
世上的人都吃了,
人人到老都不会死。

鸟雀来吃了,
鸟雀不会死;
野兽来吃了,
野兽不会死;
昆虫来吃了,
昆虫不会死……
吃过长生不老药的飞禽走兽,
熏过长生不老药的花草树木,

Who was soon cured,

And stayed healthy and immortal.

There was a little medicine left in the jar.

Everyone was invited to have a taste.

People in the east tasted it,

So they would never die.

People in the south tasted it,

So they would never die.

People in the west tasted it,

So they would never die.

People in the north tasted it,

So they would never die.

All the people in the world tasted it,

So they would not die even in old age.

Birds came to taste it,

So they would never die.

Beasts came to taste it,

So they would never die.

Insects came to taste it,

So they would never die.

Animals that had tasted the medicine

And plants that had been steamed in its vapor

查姆 // Chamu

千年都活着,
万年不会凋。

剩下的药没有煮,
剩下的药没有熬,
拿到门外晒一晒,
却被太阳月亮看见了,
太阳月亮跑下来,
偷走了长生不老药。
太阳吃了长生不老药,
太阳永远当空照。
月亮吃了长生不老药,
月亮夜晚望着大地笑。

太阳月亮偷去长生不老药,
大家心头焦。
一齐来商量,
"这药不能丢,
一定要找回这个宝。"

你搬来金柱,
我搬来银柱,
搭成天梯万丈高。
西说阿墨勒姑娘,

下部
Book Two

Stayed alive

For thousands of years.

The rest of the elixir

Was neither boiled nor stewed.

It was dried in the sun at the door.

When the sun and the moon saw it,

They ran down

And stole it.

The sun took the elixir

And was permanently shining in the sky.

The moon took the elixir

And was always smiling at the earth.

Everyone was worried that the elixir

Had been stolen by the sun and the moon.

They thought,

"The elixir should not be lost.

We must get the treasure back."

One man brought a gold pillar,

Another brought a silver pillar.

They built a sky ladder.

Xishuo'amole

拉兵也欧小伙子，
领着一只秃尾虎，
领着一只大黑狗，
上到天宫去要药苗。

忘记找白蚂蚁商量，
忘记找黄蚂蚁商量，
白蚂蚁咬断了银柱子，
黄蚂蚁咬断了金柱子。

西说阿墨勒姑娘，
拉兵也欧小伙子，
从天上掉下来，
摔死在荒郊。

老虎黑狗最先走了，
老虎黑狗上了天。
老虎要报主人恩，
天天要药苗；
太阳不给它，
它在天上吃太阳；
从此太阳有黑点，
那个老虎啃太阳。
老虎大口啃太阳的时候，

下部
Book Two

And Labingye'ou
Took a tailless tiger
And a big black dog with them,
And went to the heavenly palace
To get back the elixir.

But they forgot to tell the white ants
And the yellow ants.
The white ants chewed up the silver pillar.
The yellow ants chewed up the gold pillar.

The girl Xishuo'amole
And the boy Labinye'ou
Fell down from the sky and
Dropped to their deaths in the wilderness.

The tiger and the dog went up faster,
So they reached the sky.
The tiger, anxious to repay its owners,
Asked the sun for the elixir every day.
The sun refused to give it back,
So the tiger started to bite the sun.
From then on, there were black spots on the sun,
As the tiger kept gnawing at the sun.

那就是日食。

黑狗要报主人恩,
天天盯着月亮要药苗;
月亮不给它,
它在天上吃月亮;
请看月宫昏暗时,
那是黑狗啃月亮。
黑狗大口吃月时,
那就是月食。

彝族的祖先啊,
因为丢了长生不老药,
所以人就会老,
所以人就会死。

Book Two

When the tiger made a big bite,

A solar eclipse occurred.

The dog, anxious to repay its owners,

Asked the moon for the elixir every day.

The moon refused to give it back,

So the dog started to bite the moon.

The moon got gloomy,

Because the dog was gnawing it.

When the dog made a big bite,

A lunar eclipse occurred.

The ancestors of the Yi people

Lost the elixir.

That's why

People become old and die.

About the Translators

Xu Wei is a lecturer of English in the School of Foreign Languages and Literature at Yunnan Normal University. She was awarded the first prize in the English-speaking Tour Guides Contest held by Yunnan Tourism Bureau in 2010 and the third prize in the English-speaking Tour Guides Contest held by the State Council of China in 2010. Her recent publications include two books: *Tour-guiding in English for Colorful Yunnan* (Yunnan University Press, 2010), *Textbook for the Oral Test of English-speaking Tour Guides* (Yunnan University Press, 2016), and two articles on learning strategies for tour-guiding in English. Her research interests focus on learning and teaching strategies for tour-guiding in English, folklore translation, and cross-cultural communication.

Xiong Ying is an associate professor of English in the School of Foreign Languages and Literature at Yunnan Normal University. Her recent publications include three translations: *Scenic Regions of Yunnan* (Yunnan University Press, 1999), *Tour-guiding Yunnan in English* (Tourism & Education Publishing House, 2006), *Unique Cultural Knowledge of Yunnan Ethnic Minorities* (Yunnan University Press, 2007), and more than ten articles on education and translation. Her research interests focus on translation, multicultural education, and cross-cultural communication.

(Xu Wei translated Book Two of *Chamu* and Xiong Ying translated Book One.)